GREEN
TRIGGER
FINGERS

By the same author:

DEATH AT THE BBC

GREEN
TRIGGER
FINGERS.

JOHN SHERWOOD

CHARLES SCRIBNER'S SONS
NEW YORK

fiction
(mystery-suspense)

AUTHOR'S NOTE

The characters and events in the text are fictitious,
but with one obvious exception everything in the
footnotes is fact.

Copyright © John Sherwood 1984

Library of Congress Cataloging in Publication Data
Sherwood, John
    Green trigger fingers.
    I. Title.
PR6037.H517G7 1985   823'.914   84-10643
ISBN 0-684-18196-7

1 3 5 7 9 11 13 15 17 19   F/C   20 18 16 14 12 10 8 6 4 2

Printed in the United States of America.

1195

1 KS B + T

71560

GREEN
TRIGGER
FINGERS

ONE

"WHATEVER ARE YOU doing in there?" asked a voice from over the hedge.

What indeed, thought Celia Grant. Three years ago she had been living graciously as a wife and mother in a posh Georgian house in London. Now, unexpectedly, she was earning three pounds an hour by tidying up the neglected garden of a country cottage which had been the scene of a brutal murder.

"I'm just clipping the hedge," she replied, snipping away at the *Lonicera nitida*.

"Oh, but why?" asked Harriet Armitage, peering over the hedge into the garden of Wheelwright's Cottage. With her square face and bulging eyes she looked like a startled bullock.

"The executors are paying me to keep the scene of the tragedy tidy till they sell it," Celia explained.

"A tragedy, Celia, is when something sad happens to people of noble stature. What occurred here did not have the tragic dimension."

Celia did not comment. But it seemed to her that two people being hacked to death with an axe would not have cared whether or not they made the grade as tragedy.

"He was an accountant and she kept a hairdresser's shop," Harriet added. "They were *weekenders*, the whole thing was squalid."

Westfield was well outside the London commuter belt. Under the village's caste system the owners of weekend cottages were untouchables, like undertakers and dentists.

"Hullo, Celia," said Lucinda Fox-Norton, joining the spectators'

7

gallery in the lane. She had a lean hungry jaw, and gazed at Celia with the hostile grin of one eager to eat up Red Riding Hood bones and all.

There was a reason for this hostility, an unfortunate episode a few weeks ago. As Celia went on cutting the hedge she made up a little speech in her head about it: "Look Lucinda, I'm sorry your husband lost his head but fair's fair, it wasn't my fault, calling me an ageing mantrap was going a bit far. I didn't dye my hair when it went silver-grey, I can't help being able to eat like a horse without spoiling my figure, nor can I help being smallish and looking like some idiotic china shepherdess in need of care and protection. I'm always very firm with men who yield suddenly to their protective impulses. If you'd stayed in the garden a minute longer I'd have had him back at the far end of the sofa and all would have been well."

On second thought, it was better to leave it unsaid and let sleeping dogs lie.

Working her way along the hedge she was now opposite Lucinda, who watched her labours with disapproval. "You're wasting your time Celia. The creepier and more neglected the place looks the better, some kinky psychopath will pay a fancy price for it."

"Actually no, the agents say murder isn't a good selling point unless there's been a famous trial."

"There'll be a trial all right, when they catch young Kenny," said Harriet with relish. "Lucinda and I have been giving the Cooper woman a piece of our mind."

Celia took a needlessly savage bite out of the hedge with her electric clippers. "The Cooper woman" was Ethel Cooper who kept the village shop. Her son Kenny was the village delinquent and as he was nowhere to be found after the Emersons' murder he was widely supposed to have hacked them to death with their own wood-axe.

"She's hiding that son of hers from the police," said Harriet. "Don't look at me like that, Celia, you know it's true."

Unfortunately for Celia, her china-doll features were too

8

expressive, her face was like a computer screen on which her thoughts were thrown up for all to read. It was displaying deep dismay, for she was facing a moment of crisis. Since settling in Westfield she had tried to steer a neutral course in village politics, which were as complicated and almost as violent as those of a Central American republic. This was only possible by keeping very quiet, but there was a limit to what one could refrain from saying, and it had now been reached.

"Ethel Cooper's a friend of mine," she protested.

"That woman is *evil*," said Harriet.

Lucinda nodded. "She knows where that boy of hers is and she's sending him money."

"How can you be so sure?" asked Celia. There was no evidence at all to prove this allegation, yet Harriet and Lucinda had been broadcasting it all round the village in their penetrating upper-class voices, to the indignation of the peasantry.

"Of course we're sure," said Harriet. "The whole thing was a blot on the village, and we all know it was the Cooper woman's fault, hers and that trendy-lefty social worker's."

"They were far too soft with her precious Kenny, and look what happened," said Lucinda, snapping her lantern jaw.

Celia had a sudden vision of Harriet and Lucinda dangling from lampposts outside the pub and being pelted with rotten fruit by the angry proletariat. Censoring this thought suitably, she said, "Ethel's very popular, you know."

"Not among People Like Us," said Harriet firmly.

"Oh, but you shouldn't make accusations you can't prove against people who can't afford to answer back."

Harriet's look withered her as a class traitor. "You sound very left wing suddenly, Celia, there's an unpleasant underdoggy flavour about you."

At this Celia let fly. "If you're not careful people will begin to suspect that you're pointing the finger at Kenny Cooper to divert attention from the real culprit, because you know that the Emersons were chopped up by some well-bred Person Like Us."

There was an awful silence, like the interval between the

lightning and the thunder. "How dare you?" croaked Harriet as the veins in her neck swelled with rage.

"That is an infamous suggestion," snapped Lucinda.

"You're the one who should be careful," Harriet went on. "There is such a thing as slander."

The two matrons withdrew down the lane, telling each other that Celia was getting very odd, no doubt as a result of living alone, and one knew about her and *men*.

Maybe I am getting odd, Celia thought. What a way to behave, I must have been mad. The episode on the Fox-Nortons' sofa was bad enough, and now she had well and truly cooked her goose, made enemies for good of Harriet's bridge-playing coterie as well as Lucinda's crop of horse-fanciers. She had said far more than was wise in a village whose chief industry was gossip. Mercifully she had not lost her temper, which she knew made her look ridiculous, like the Queen of the Fairies having a tantrum.

A reaction had set in. It was true what they said, living alone made these moments of depression worse. Getting her balance after a crisis had never been a problem when Roger was alive, he had been marvellous at bringing down her misery-quotient, as he called it, when it got too high. But Roger was dead and her children away from home. He had been a leading light on the staff of the Royal Botanic Gardens at Kew, and on top of his other virtues the funniest man she had ever met. Various replacements had offered themselves, for her hair had gone silver-grey before its time and she was still appetising. But none of them had been acceptable as a substitute for Roger, so she had started a small horticultural business to fill up the gap in her life.

When she had finished clipping the hedge she prepared to carry out a tricky operation which always made her wish she was a large and beefy man. A nineteen-inch mower with a heavy roller had to be got down out of her van. Her method was to lower it down a slope consisting of planks which she carried in the van for the purpose. Having performed this feat, which required nerve and muscle, she mowed the lawn and considered what to do next in fulfilment of her maintenance contract. The flowerbeds were full

10

of bindweed and the irises needed dividing, but this dreadful garden would not be her responsibility much longer, so she pulled the tops off the more conspicuous weeds and trimmed the edges of the beds. Neatly trimmed grass edges were more noticeable than a mere absence of weeds and convinced clients that they were getting their money's worth. For good measure she dead-headed some short-stemmed early irises. Their flowers had withered into claw-like stumps of dingy yellow and grey which always reminded her of something unpleasant. What? The feet of horrid boiled chickens, perhaps.

The tubs on the terrace needed water. As she filled the can at the tap by the back door it opened and a sheep-like little grey-haired woman in glasses looked out. A tall balding man with a long nose was peering over her shoulder.

"Hullo," said Celia. "I'm Celia Grant, how d'you do?"

Their name, it seemed, was Hanley. They had just bought Wheelwright's Cottage and were measuring it for curtains. Celia had heard their car scrunch over the gravel and stop, but had been too busy to investigate. She produced suitable words of welcome.

"It seems such a peaceful, friendly village," said Mrs Hanley. "We're retiring, and it'll be lovely to get away from all those nasty muggings and so on in London and live where things like that don't happen."

Celia tried not to look aghast. Did they not realise that less than a month ago the spot where they were standing, just outside the back door, had been the scene of a very messy double murder? Had they not wondered about the ridiculously low price they were paying for an Elizabethan cottage, modernised within an inch of its life, in a gilt-edged beauty spot village with access to a fast train service to London?

Mr Hanley was looking uncomfortable. "Actually, Vera . . ." he began. So they did know.

"Oh, that," said Mrs Hanley firmly. "We agreed not to talk about it or even think about it, didn't we, Edward dear? I expect you knew them, Mrs er . . ."

"Grant," said Celia. "I didn't know them at all well."

11

"But the Emersons were only weekenders, weren't they? I'm told they didn't mix."

"They spent very little time here. They were business people from London."

"What sort of business?"

"Something very ordinary and dull. I'm sure you're wise to think and talk about them as little as possible."

"That's what I told Edward. If we don't talk about it people will soon forget. It's not as if the Emersons were local, and what happened to them was nothing to do with the village."

Celia checked her mounting dismay. It would be cruel to disillusion them before they had settled in, they would find out their mistake soon enough.

"I must be moving on, I'd more or less finished," she said. "I'll just collect my tools."

"Oh, you've been mowing the grass for us, how kind," said Mrs Hanley.

"Not really. I run a small horticultural business, I'm being paid to keep the garden tidy by the solicitors acting for the estate."

At this news Mrs Hanley looked at Celia's well-worn gardening clothes and seemed to be worrying about where to place her socially. Her husband pointed his long nose at a neglected tangle of shrubs, as if to suggest that the solicitors were not having their money's worth.

"Tch, tch," he remarked.

"Yes, there's a lot of dead wood in there," Celia agreed. "But the contract's only for four hours a week and I haven't had time to do much pruning."

"You can safely leave that to me," he said. "I wonder if you realise that this sadly neglected garden is full of rarities. There's even a *Cornus nuttallii* over there, let me show you."

Celia followed him politely down one of the niggly little grass paths which snaked about in the tangle of overgrown fancy shrubbery. The garden had been laid out by the Emersons' predecessor. He had stuffed it with fast-growing subjects planted too close together and had moved out in despair when the result began to look like vegetable science fiction.

Celia waited in a small clearing while Mr Hanley crashed about in the undergrowth, scattering Latin names at random. He was classifiable botanically as a member of the semi-knowledgeable group, sub-genus show off, a species she usually tolerated, but this was getting embarrassing. Presently they faced each other over a dreary little green bush with a few small white flowers.

"*Osmanthus delavayi*," he proclaimed, pointing at it.

"Actually I'm afraid it isn't, it's *Osmarea burkwoodii*. You'll see if you have another look at the leaf. People often confuse the two."

"Really? I wonder if you can possibly be right, but oh dear, here we have *Euphorbia robbiae*. Very invasive, a real nuisance."

"Yes. One sometimes wishes she hadn't put it in her hatbox."

"I beg your pardon?"

"She was going plant-collecting in Turkey, and she took a very imposing hat with her to impress the pashas with, and on the way back she saw this hitherto unrecorded euphorbia growing somewhere near Istanbul and scooped it up. But there wasn't anywhere else to put it in her luggage, so she threw out the hat which had served its purpose . . ."

"Excuse me, who are you talking about?"

"Oh, I'm sorry. Mrs Robb.* That's why it's called *Euphorbia robbiae*."

Unabashed by this display of knowledge Mr Hanley looked about him eagerly. "Rescuing this garden will be tremendously exciting."

"Before you do anything else," Celia suggested anxiously, "you ought to repair that fence. If I were you I'd put barbed wire along the top too."

"In time. There is so much to do."

"Oh, but you must take this seriously. Your garden backs on ten acres of unfenced woodland. When your cottage is burgled, which

*For further details of this remarkable woman, see *Journal* of the Royal Horticultural Society, July 1973, p. 306. The late A.E. Bowles nicknamed her plant "Mrs Robb's Bonnet".

happens three or four times a year, the standard approach route is through that wood, which is called Butler's Copse. Then they come over the fence and up to the back of the house."

Mr Hanley digested this and sobered down. Suddenly his eyes filled with alarm. "Is that how the Emersons. . . ?"

Celia hesitated.

"Please, Mrs Grant. I have to know."

"Oh dear, I wasn't going to tell you, but—yes. The Emersons disturbed a burglar, who killed them because they recognised him."

"But . . . that's pure speculation, you can't possibly know. The agents told us definitely that the mystery had never been cleared up."

"Not officially, nothing was ever proved. But the police are sure that's what happened."

"You don't mean, they know who the murderer was?"

Celia hesitated. "Let's say there's one strong suspect. If you encourage village gossip you'll soon hear all the details."

"But you're implying that he's a local man."

"That's what people here think."

"Surely not. What you're saying runs counter to everything the agents told us. They assured us that all the signs pointed to gang warfare of some kind in London."

"No. According to the police the Emersons lived a blameless life in London, quite unremarkable. All the circumstances suggested a burglary that went wrong."

He gazed at her for a moment with a horrified expression, then crashed off through the undergrowth shouting "Vera! Vera!" Presently sounds of recrimination came from the cottage. ". . . I said we ought to make more enquiries. . . . You were the one who was in such a hurry . . ."

Celia felt very sorry for the Hanleys. Tempted by a bargain price they had decided, wrongly, that they were hard-boiled enough to ignore what had happened at Wheelwright's, and to make things worse they were obviously ill-equipped for survival amid the subtleties and pitfalls of village life. When they had settled in she would have to do what she could to help.

14

She collected her tools and got the mower back into the van, which was easier than getting it out if one started the motor and drove it boldly up the sloping planks. With a goodbye to the Hanleys she left them to their consternation and drove off up the lane to the village.

Westfield's village street was a show-piece, a jumble of red-roofed houses and cottages built over a spread of five centuries on no particular plan, which had mellowed into a coherent master-piece. What delighted Celia was the front gardens, all well-kept. Village opinion frowned heavily on weeds and neglected grass. Some of the layouts were charming, others seemed to her dreadful mistakes, and this year she really would suggest to the landlord of the Westfield Arms that pink geraniums in the window-boxes would look better than scarlet against red brick. Her special favourite was a little fenced square the size of a child's playpen outside a tiny cottage. It was always a gorgeous muddle of simple cottage flowers.

When she drew up outside the village shop she was waylaid by the doctor's wife, begging for plants for her plant stall in aid of the Hospice for the Dying. As this would put the doctor's wife under a moral obligation to bake a cake for Celia's Save the Children Fund, Celia agreed. But she could not escape till she had been brought up to date with the latest developments concerning the factional strife in the Village Hall Committee, the umbrage over the Red Cross coffee morning, and the row over the solar heating panels on the Isaacsons' fifteenth-century roof.

It seemed to Celia that the village had never been in such a state, and to cap it all the peasantry, who normally regarded the People Like Us as a good joke, had been infuriated by Harriet and Lucinda's hate campaign against Ethel Cooper. At this rate too few people would be on speaking terms to get the church fête off the ground. Something must be done to calm them all down. She would creep round the village in the early morning putting Valium in all the milk bottles. Disguised as the milkman's boy, perhaps, without his knowledge. But one had to be a bosomy soprano in an opera to get away with that.

15

Snapping out of this fantasy she unloaded from the van the orders of autumn-flowering saxifrages and cyclamen that she had packed that morning ready to post off to customers. The village shop, a rabbit-warren of low-ceilinged rooms full of groceries, had a Post Office counter in one corner.

"How's business, Ethel?" she asked as she handed the packages over. Such enquiries were in order, for Ethel treated her as a fellow shopkeeper. This was one of the things she liked about her position in the village; as a working gardener she could pass from the drawing rooms of the People Like Us to a farm labourer's kitchen and still be treated as an equal.

"Business is shocking, dear," said Ethel.

Harriet and Lucinda and their cronies had mounted a boycott of the village shop to punish Ethel for letting her son besmirch the village with a sordid murder. The boycott was confined to the gentry, but they were the main customers. The peasantry preferred to push their groaning trolleys through the supermarkets in Haxton, the nearest town, and Ethel had perforce gone up-market. When emergency or forgetfulness forced the peasantry into her shop they were scandalised by the prices, but they were solidly on her side against Harriet and Lucinda.

"You still haven't heard from Kenny?" Celia asked.

Ethel became slightly tearful. "No dear. He can read a bit but he never got the hang of writing, otherwise he would. Those poor Emersons, he'd never do a thing like that but he knew the police would pick on him, they always do. That's why he run away."

This account of the matter omitted one awkward fact. Everyone including the police knew that Kenny had a habit of breaking into Wheelwright's Cottage during the week when it was empty. If he was innocent of the murder he nevertheless had a strong motive for making himself scarce. Celia was fairly sure that Ethel genuinely did not know where he was.

"That Mrs Fox-Norton's just been in," said Ethel, "and Mrs Armitage."

"Yes. They told me."

"Doing a cross-talk act behind the tinned fruit, all about how I

16

knew where Kenny was hiding and how I was sending him money on the quiet. At the top of their voices too, so I'd hear."

"Oh really, why didn't you throw them out of the shop?"

"You can't talk to those people dear, they can't help it, it's the way they were brought up. I'd sell and get out if I could, but who'd look at it with the turnover figures I've had? I'll have the shutters up if this goes on much longer."

"Oh no," said Celia anxiously. The village school had closed, there were no buses except on Thursdays—if the shop collapsed too, Westfield would be one step nearer becoming a beauty-spot museum. Even the church was down to two services a month from a vicar three villages away who behaved like the Victorian music-hall artistes, dashing from one London theatre to another in a cab to repeat their number.

"I tried to shut those two awful women up," Celia went on. "I told them if they went on much longer about you and Kenny people would begin to think they were covering up for someone."

Ethel looked surprised and distressed. "Oh Celia dear, how did you know, who told you?"

"No one, I just said it to keep them quiet."

"1 wish you hadn't dear, it's all round the village and I try to stop people repeating it, it'll only make things worse for me."

"You mean, there's something in it?"

Before she could answer the shop bell tinkled. Ethel busied herself with Celia's packets of plants. Three people had come in, so the subject had to be dropped for the present. Celia left the shop thoughtfully. Perhaps there was nothing in it, it would be typical of Westfield politics if the village had decided to point suspicion at the gentry as a class-warfare ploy in support of Ethel.

Wondering about this, she drove back to Archerscroft, the cottage with two acres of land which she had bought after Roger's death to set up her nursery garden.

This venture had been Roger's idea. During his long terminal illness his main concern had been for the future she would have to face without him. He had foreseen that she would be utterly at a loss to find a new role after two decades and more as a wife and

17

mother. Her own mind was a blank, except for a determination not to prey on their three children, all out in the world and starting their careers. He had gradually led her to the idea of a small nursery specialising in good garden plants threatened with extinction; charming old-fashioned things that the big nurseries, geared to volume production for the mass market, could not be bothered with, because demand was too small or they were too difficult to propagate.

It had been tough at first, especially having to make decisions without consulting Roger. She soon found that the horticultural scene had changed rapidly, the area that the commercial nurseries and garden centres had withdrawn from was being filled by a host of enthusiastic amateurs and semi-professionals who were running businesses just like her own from their private gardens. Competition was fierce, but she had worked hard and been lucky. Her bordered cottage pinks and auriculas sold well by mail order, there was money in the rarer hostas, and one of her hellebores, a cross between *corsicus* and *niger*, had won a commendation at the Royal Horticultural Society spring show in London. Her trading loss in the first year had been terrifying and she had taken on the garden maintenance contracts to keep the business solvent while stocks were built up and sales outlets found. By now she was breaking even and to her surprise was enjoying herself. Having married and started a family young, she was having a career for the first time. It astonished her to find that she was quite good at it.

The half-timbered yeoman's cottage on the property dated from the fourteenth century and was called Archerscroft from the belief of a previous owner that two massive yews in the front garden must have been planted to provide bow-shafts for the longbowmen of the Hundred Years' War. It stood in a narrow lane a mile from the village and she grudged the space needed for a car park inside the gate. She parked the van by the packing shed and went into the frame yard, where Deirdre Foster was doing the afternoon watering. She was Celia's assistant, taken on when the garden maintenance contracts became unmanageable for one. She was thin and restless, with dark brown eyes and a blank face that

18

gave no clue as to what went on in her mind. One gathered that her childless marriage was unsatisfactory.

She straightened as Celia approached. "I say, come and look at this. I noticed it just now when I started watering the cold frames."

Celia looked, and saw a large and startlingly handsome primrose. The scarlet flowers were fully double, with a shocking-pink edge to every petal. "Goodness, where on earth did that spring from?"

Presently she remembered. On a holiday in Ireland she had collected a rose-pink double primrose from a neglected cottage garden and brought it home. Being double it had no female organs and could not reproduce itself sexually. But it seemed unable to believe this and kept throwing flower after flower in a frantic attempt to have progeny. It managed however to produce a surprising amount of pollen and Celia, rather than waste it, had used it to pollinate various other primroses she happened to have around. As a result of this casual experiment in plant-breeding it had fathered a dozen seedlings, of which this was the first to flower. Four more were in bud.

"Isn't it exciting?" said Deirdre.

"Yes, but it can't have any offspring. It's double."

"Some of the flowers are only semi-double. Look."

Celia picked up the pot. Deirdre was right. Two of the blooms were proudly displaying a complete set of male and female organs. Pistils and stamens were equally prominent, so that unlike ordinary primroses this one would be self-fertile. If the others were all the same they would breed like rabbits with little assistance from her.

"You can take out plant-breeder's rights and make a fortune," said Deirdre.

This was unlikely, apart from the fact that plant breeder's rights were no goldmine. Even semi-double primroses seldom came true from seed, and the next generation would almost certainly be a brood of singles in various colours. Several specialist nurseries had experimented with double primroses and failed, scratching away among the masses of petals for the few grains of pollen that they sometimes produced, and teasing away offsets to keep the strain going when they failed to set seed. But she might just have struck it lucky and had to feel a little excited. Everyone wanted a double primrose, knowing it was something rare that most people could not have.

"Now I'll tell you the bad news," said Deirdre. "Ron phoned. He's at The Towers. His mower's broken down."

Ron was the latest in a succession of semi-skilled youths hired to cut grass.

"What's wrong with it?" Celia asked.

"I don't know, but he says it won't go and he can't get it up into the van by himself."

Celia wished she had been told this earlier. In a few minutes Ron would be sitting by a broken-down mower on overtime.

"We'll both have to go," she decided, getting back into the driving seat. Ron was skinny and undersized. It would take the three of them to haul the dead weight of a nineteen-inch mower up the sloping planks into the back of the van.

As they drove to The Towers she told Deirdre about her shouting match over the hedge with Harriet and Lucinda.

"You mean, they're deliberately manufacturing this outcry against Ethel and Kenny Cooper to shield someone else?" Deirdre asked.

"It needn't have been them. Someone must have started the thing and they all took it up like dogs at night, one of them barks and then they all begin without knowing why."

At the end of the village street she turned right along the edge of Butler's Copse, then right again into the long rhododendron-lined drive of The Towers. She parked in the yard behind the gaunt Victorian house and they set off on foot to find Ron.

The garden here was neglected, but on the grand scale. There were eleven acres of it, glade after glade lined with rare shrubs and trees, mostly sixty or more years old. It had been planted by a distinguished traveller and plant collector who had died aged ninety after his discoveries among the flora of the Chinese-Tibetan border had made horticultural history and earned him a knighthood. His arthritic gardener had soon followed him into the grave and the widow had closed thankfully with Celia's offer to maintain the garden on contract. The work was mainly grass-cutting, since the exotic shrubs and trees were mostly well enough established to look after themselves. But she could do nothing with the large outlying areas which the tottery gardener had allowed to become scruffy.

They found Ron down on the lower lawn, out of sight of the house, sitting smoking behind his broken-down mower. The damage to it proved serious. One of the blades had a huge bite out of it. The chain had jammed and sheared the cotter pin on the drive shaft. There were only two mowers. They would have merry hell covering the contracts with one during the repairs.

"How on earth did that happen?" Celia asked.

"Stone," said Ron.

"I told you to look out for stones."

"I did. Couldn't see it, it was in the grahnd."

"Show me."

It was a piece of ragstone, quite large and half buried in the turf. Fragments from the impact were scattered in the path of the mower.

"There's another big bit here," said Deirdre, poking about in the grass.

Where had they come from? The garden was on greensand, with a layer of acid-to-neutral loam as topsoil. There had once been a farm on the site and one sometimes came across the foundations of buildings, but only three feet or more down. Assuming that bits of stone had somehow worked their way to the surface, how had they got imbedded in the grass? Trodden in during the winter, no doubt, while the turf was spongy, but who by? On fine days the old lady in the house sometimes hobbled round the garden on two sticks, but no one else took the slightest interest in it. Certainly, no one but Celia and her staff had worked in it.

The mower had come to grief a few yards from one of the few herbaceous borders that had not been grassed down to save work. Celia looked at it. It was a June-to-September border, with some irises to start it off in May. But here was another puzzle. Something was wrong with the irises. . . .

What else was in the border? Day lilies and lupins and delphiniums, all showing quite a lot of leaf already, so were the phloxes, nothing was wrong with any of them apart from a little slug damage on the delphiniums. But those irises. . . .

"Deirdre. The irises. Look!"

"What about them?"

"The intermediates and the others are all mixed up. We didn't leave them like that!"

There were two sorts of iris in the bed, she remembered, both in mixed colours. When they dug it through in the autumn they had carefully kept the intermediates that flowered in May separate from the tall June-flowering ones, so that they could replant them in separate clumps with the short intermediates near the front. Now they were all in mixed clumps, tall and short together. The intermediates were already in bud.

Who would have thought that in late spring with nothing in flower yet, a herbaceous border could look faintly sinister?

"And what on earth are those bare patches?" said Celia. There were two big blank patches of earth where nothing was coming through.

"Something's missing," she decided. "There must have been something in there to flower after the lupins and delphiniums and keep the colour going till the phloxes and day lilies took over."

She shut her eyes and tried to see the border as it had been the previous summer. "Alstromerias! There were two big clumps where the bare patches are. They ought to be through by now."

She stepped into the bed for a closer look. But there was no sign of the grey-green leaves which would normally be thrusting through the soil. Alstromerias disappeared completely during the winter. The filament-like roots were very brittle and attempts to transplant them usually killed them unless one was very careful. A non-gardener with a spade could destroy them without even knowing they were there.

Whoever had done this was a gardener of sorts. He knew how to

22

plant irises with the rhizome facing the sun, but thought all irises were the same size and flowered at the same time. He did not know about alstromerias. He had dug over six or eight feet of the border and replanted it to the best of his ability. Why? To bury something?

A chilling suspicion made the back of her neck prickle. It all fitted. Wheelwright's Cottage was only a few hundred yards away on the other side of Butler's Copse. Something had been buried in the flowerbed, and she knew what it was.

Correction. Not what. Who.

TWO

HALF CELIA'S BRAIN insisted that ten minutes with a spade would reveal the gruesome remains of Kenny Cooper. The other half told her that this was melodramatic nonsense. Her inner chaos must have shown in her face, for Deirdre was staring at her. The dark eyes which told one nothing were boring into her, trying to read her thoughts.

But Ron was on overtime and the first priority was to get the broken-down mower into one of the vans. "Then you can go home, Ron. You too, Deirdre. I'll finish the grass with the other mower."

"Aren't you going to do something about it?" Deirdre asked.

"About what?"

"The border. To find out why it's been messed up."

"I might dig around a bit. You get off home, you know what a fuss your Timothy makes if his meal's a bit late."

Ron grinned. "Think there's a body buried under there, do yer?"

Celia cursed herself, why did her thoughts have to show up on her face? And now she was beginning to blush.

"You get off home, Ron," she said roughly.

The idea was absurd, she realised when they had gone. Who would bury a body in a flowerbed with Butler's Copse just over the fence and miles of open country to choose from as well? Why fiddle with a lot of irises and stuff in someone's garden?

Before she could take comfort from this thought, the unwelcome answer to her own question came to her. It was obvious, one had only to think back over the events of the previous month or two, to

24

something that had happened . . . yes, it must have been about the same time as the row over the Isaacsons' solar heating panels, which dated it about a week before the Emersons were hacked to pieces with their own axe. That was when the youngest daughter of the problem family down at the Piggeries had gone missing. Nobody knew then that her mentally defective uncle had taken her off on a spree to London without telling anyone, and volunteers had been helping the police to search woods and waste ground. Freshly disturbed soil anywhere within miles of Westfield would attract attention as soon as it was found.

Except in a flowerbed in a remote corner of a garden which had already been thoroughly searched.

There was one other possibility. What if a guest at The Towers needing exercise had been let loose in the garden with a spade? She must check in the house.

The Towers was a formidable pile of Victorian grey brick, and justified the use of the plural by having a staircase turret as well as the tall main tower topped by a kind of gazebo with openings on all four sides from which to admire the view. The house had the same air of grand neglect as the garden. Dingy blinds or ramshackle shutters blocked the windows on the upper floors which were uninhabited. Old Lady Armitage could no longer manage the stairs and slept in what had once been the breakfast room.

Celia rang the bell and waited in the cavernous porch. Mrs Box, the cook and only survivor of a once-numerous staff, was eighty and slow-moving. She would take time to drag herself to the front hall, switch off the burglar alarm and unchain the door.

"Hullo, Boxie," said Celia when this happened. "I'd like a word with Lady Armitage."

Mrs Box, who liked Celia, grinned toothlessly. "Come in, dearie, and I'll see."

The hall was cluttered with brass gongs, elephants' tusks and heavily carved oriental furniture, the by-products of Sir Henry's plant collecting expeditions to the Far East. A bamboo plant stand held a stunning display of cinerarias in vivid colours, from cyclamen pink to the darkest midnight purple. These were the

25

work of Lady Armitage's daughter Alison and represented a real achievement. Cinerarias were tricky and needed constant spraying for aphis.

Mrs Box opened a door flanked by huge Chinese jars containing scarlet clivias, also Alison's work. "Miss Alison," she shouted.

"What is it, Boxie?"

"It's Miz Grant. Wants ter see 'er ladyship."

Footsteps. Alison Fitzgerald appeared, a colourless fifty-year-old made even more colourless by a faded linen dress. Her only expression of personality was her greenhouse. Perhaps the violent colours of the cinerarias and clivias were a form of compensation. She had married late and impulsively, and had been driven back home by the failure of a disastrous union.

Celia was deeply sorry for Alison, who looked after the old lady and the domesticities of a wildly inconvenient house with no help except Boxie's. It was a scandal that she got none whatever from Harriet Armitage, her sister-in-law.

"I'll just see if mother's awake," said Alison, and went back the way she had come.

Calling on the old lady was always like this. Boxie dismantled the defences and let one in, then handed one over to Alison, who always had to "go and see". Sometimes one had to wait ten minutes or more before being admitted to the presence chamber, and Celia often wondered what went on during this waiting period. She had never been allowed to walk straight in.

This time Alison reappeared quickly. "Yes, do come in," she said, as if conferring an unheard-of privilege. Celia followed her across a comfortless drawing room, seemingly unused except as a parking place for yet more cinerarias and as a last line of defence before the presence chamber. At the far end Alison knocked on a door (but why after all this palaver was it necessary to knock?) and ushered Celia into the old lady's sitting room, which contained no cinerarias whatever.

"Celia, how nice of you to come," said Lady Armitage.

"Hullo, Nellie."

Celia could never believe that Nellie Armitage and her daughter were blood relations. Even at eighty-two Nellie was mischievously pretty, with sparkling blue eyes and enough charm to sink a battleship. Moreover she was tiny. How on earth had she managed to produce a listless lump of womanhood twice her size?

"Sit down, Celia dear, sit down. Alison, go and get her some tea."

Celia was in no mood for a leisurely social call and refused tea, whereupon Alison sat down promptly to mount guard. Too late, Celia realised that refusing tea was a false move, for Alison was a permanent mass of nerves. Alarming topics were taboo in her presence, though the fiction was maintained that they must be avoided in case they "upset mother". Before enquiries could be made about the herbaceous border means must be found to get her out of the room.

"D'you know anything about double primroses, Nellie?" Celia asked with this end in view.

"Yes, why?"

Celia described the result of her plant-breeding experiment with the primroses. "The awful thing is, I can't repeat the cross because I don't remember what I used for the seed parents. I think I threw most of them away. But the one that's in flower looks as if it's going to be self-fertile."

"The next generation will probably be a brood of singles," Nellie predicted, then mused for a moment. "Woman I knew in America called Florence Bellis, lived in Oregon, she used to grow the doubles.* Never made much of it though, they're tricky. Alison, get me my American portfolio."

According to plan, Alison went. She would be away for five minutes at least. Up on the first floor behind closed shutters was Sir Henry Armitage's library and herbarium, a superb collection of botanical books and dried specimens. Also kept up there was Nellie's life work, for she had followed him from the mountains of China to the rain-forests of Peru doing exquisite botanical drawings of the plants he collected.

*The double primroses raised by Florence Bellis of Gresham, Oregon, were known as the Barnhaven strain. For the elaborate back-crossing needed to grow them from seed, see R.H.S. *Journal*, September 1971, p390.

As Alison disappeared, Celia said, "By the way, has anyone been working in the garden during the winter? Apart from me and Deirdre?"

"Not that I know of dear. Why?"

Celia told her about the irises and the alstromerias, deliberately making the story as flat and undramatic as possible. "I wondered if someone had an energetic fit and did some digging. Alison, perhaps."

Nellie let out a cackle of laughter. "Her? Digging? Oh no dear, she's exhausted by mid-morning from the effort of bullying me and de-lousing those damn cinerarias."

"D'you mind then, if I rummage about a bit with a spade and see what's what?"

"Of course, do what you like," said Nellie and launched out into the usual complaints of the elderly against those who look after them.

"You're a naughty old tease, the way you treat her," Celia interrupted. "If she ran away and told you to go to hell it would serve you right."

"She can't, no money. I do try to behave, but she brings out the beast in me. So bloody meek, nervous as a seasick cat too. Don't tell her you think there's a body under there or she'll have a fit."

Nellie's skill as a mind-reader was a shock. "Nothing so exciting, I'm sure," Celia murmured.

"You're right," said Nellie, studying her shrewdly. "Who'd risk burying a body in a herbaceous border with miles of open country to choose from?"

Behind her the door to the hall had swung open. "What's that?" cried Alison, advancing into the room. "What's that about a body?"

Nellie looked at her severely. "We were only joking, Alison you goose. Give me that thing."

Alison was carrying an artist's portfolio tied with tape.

"Ah, let's see," said Nellie, seizing it. "The primroses are all together at the back. Yes, here you are Celia."

Nellie was a born artist. Her drawings were botanically

28

accurate—Sir Henry would have given her hell if they were not. But they were also beautifully disposed on the page and showed the character of the plant as well as its botanical detail. Celia was in no mood to dally and had seen the portfolio before, but she had in decency to admire a dozen exquisitely drawn pages of double primroses raised by Florence Bellis in the nineteen forties and fifties. None of them resembled the rose-pink father of the brood in the cold frame.

"If it does come true from seed, which I doubt," said Nellie, "you'll make quite a lot of money."

"And Roger will be gnashing his teeth up in heaven. He hated overbred double flowers. *Kerria japonica* made him froth at the mouth."

"Quite right dear, filthy thing. William Kerr was a drunken little bastard by all accounts, got into bad company out east.* Probably too high on *saké* to see what a nasty plant he was collecting."

Celia could see Roger now, grimacing hideously and muttering curses at a straggling kerria in her father's garden which had just produced its shapeless yellow blobs of petals with no working parts. It was at moments like this that being a widow suddenly hurt.

Alison, who had been simmering like a kettle during this discussion, now came to the boil. "Mother, what were you and Celia talking about just now when I came in?"

"Nothing of any importance, dear."

"You keep things from me. I insist on knowing."

There was a taut silence. Alison's frightened stare switched from Nellie to Celia and back again. It was unfortunate, she had obviously heard too much.

"I must go and finish your grass," said Celia, rising.

---

*Nellie was being unfair to Kerr, a brilliantly successful plant collector. He clashed temperamentally with his superior in the East India Company, whose adverse reports home of loose behaviour were probably ill-founded. The shrub he introduced was of course the double variety. The charming single kerria, which is the type plant, was not introduced into Britain until about 1835.

"Must you dear? Alison, let her out, then bring me a whisky, a proper one. Not your usual gnat's piss and water."

"Very well, Mother."

"Her trouble's constipation," said Lady Armitage. "Goodbye, Celia dear."

Alison led the way back to the front hall.

"You ought to stand up to her more," said Celia. "If you behave like a doormat she'll treat you as one."

"You don't realise how difficult it is." Alison was almost in tears and her hand trembled as she reached out to switch off the burglar alarm.

"Goodness, is that really necessary in the daytime?" Celia asked.

"Of course it is! Three women alone in an isolated house like this! With Butler's Copse all round us and that dreadful Wheelwright's Cottage the other end of it! A man came to the door the other day, a real ruffian, asking if we had any antiques to sell, if you please. I didn't even take the chain off the door."

The burglar alarm in the daytime was a recent development; Alison was getting into a really bad state. It was lucky The Towers had no drawbridge, or she would have had Boxie cranking it up and down every time anyone rang the bell.

Round the corner of the house Celia unloaded her mower from the van and set out with it towards the lower lawn. Her route passed through the stable yard. As usual a selection of Nigel Fitzgerald's sculptures was displayed in it. He was Alison's son by her disastrous marriage. The coach house was his studio and he lived in the flat above it: no doubt he had to be outside Alison's defensive perimeter for the sake of his love life. Recently he had been "into" plastic tubing, but that period seemed to be over. He was now working on discarded bits of motorcars by way of satirical comment on the restless throwaway society. Avoiding several compositions along these lines Celia got her mower down to the lower lawn and finished cutting the grass. Then she began to dig.

Whoever disturbed the bed had gone deep. She was still finding

30

fragments of alstromeria root two feet down. The trees had begun to cast long shadows over the lawn.

"Working late?" asked a man's voice.

She looked up. Another long shadow slanted across the lawn. Nigel's.

He was another genetic puzzle, tall and lean and very dark, with a permanent secret smile. The Armitages did not come true to seed, for he was quite unlike his mother or grandmother. Perhaps he took after his male parent, like her primrose.

"I saw you pass, I was upstairs in the flat," he said. "What did you think of my new sculptures?"

"To be honest, I think they're too big for living rooms and not well enough finished for trendy museums. You ought to do little models of them in brass, like those scale models of old-fashioned railway engines. They'd sell."

Typically Nigel made no comment apart from maintaining his secret smile. "Are you going to plant a tree in that enormous hole?"

"No, there's a theory that something's been buried here. Your grandmother jokingly suggests a body." Doubt welled up again and she added, "But that's absurd."

"Yes. Why risk a flowerbed in a garden with the whole countryside to choose from?"

Celia did not answer.

"I suppose it makes for easier digging. No tree roots or rocks or heavy clay to hold you up. If you've got a body and no flowerbed you have to burst your guts with a pickaxe or put it in one of those shallow graves that the police always find."

He watched her dig for several minutes. "I wonder who it is? No one actually got killed at the Red Cross coffee morning, but what about the Village Hall Committee?"

"No blood was shed there as far as I know."

"Puzzling." He turned, still smiling secretly. "I shall go back indoors and decide who I hope it is."

Presently Celia stopped digging to rest her back. The sun was already low behind Butler's Copse. The far end of it, where

31

Wheelwright's Cottage stood behind its broken-down fence, was already in darkness. Soon after she started digging again she noticed the smell. It had become a nauseating stench by the time she came across the shoe. It was attached to something, but rotten. When pulled it disintegrated. Part of a mouldering sock came away with it, to reveal Kenny Cooper's toes.

THREE

IN HER HURRY she dialled 999 without noticing that there was no
dialling tone. A second attempt established that her phone was
dead. Her nearest neighbour, an elderly bachelor a quarter of a
mile away, took an eternity to answer the door.

"Could I use your phone please to ring the police? Mine's out of
order."

"The police?"

"Yes. I'll explain later."

"If you want to ring them about the fire, Mrs Grant, I expect
they know already."

Only then did she notice the red glow behind the trees, low down
in the night sky. "Where is it?"

"Barton Farm. Only a haystack, I'm told, but it's burnt through
the overhead cables. All the telephones in the village are cut off,
including yours and mine."

Barton Farm was down on the busy main road to London. A
fire with smoke billowing across the dual carriageway would cause
a traffic problem. The police would be there.

They were, and so were various other emergency services, blue
and amber lights flashed everywhere. Celia counted four fire
engines, a lot for a mere haystack fire. But the haystack was
alarmingly close to some farm cottages, not to speak of the
milking sheds and an ancient wooden barn full of expensive farm
machinery. The fire engines were blocking one of the carriageways.
On the other the police were struggling with a huge tailback of
Friday night traffic to the coast. Celia parked on the verge and
walked forward to speak to one of them.

33

"Keep back there please lady, we can't have sightseers."

"Oh but I'm not a sightseer, I want to report a murder. I've found a body in a flowerbed."

"Sorry lady, what was that?" he said abstractedly, waving his arms and keeping his eyes fixed on the traffic.

She began to explain haltingly, but he went on hurrying the stream of traffic past him. Having heard enough with half an ear to doubt if she was sane, he interrupted her. "Look lady, I've got me hands full here. Why don't you go home and dial 999."

"Because all the phones in the village are cut off."

"There's a public one down the road, at the roundabout by Hodson's Garden Centre. That'll be okay."

It was like one of those hurry-dreams in which some vital objective cannot be reached because of an ever-changing nightmare of irrelevant obstacles. Having run back to where she had parked the van she had to sit frustrated for what seemed like hours in a queue of traffic waiting to pass the blockage. On reaching the phone box at the roundabout she ransacked her purse for money, and took some time to remember that emergency calls were free.

This time her story was taken seriously. "Where are you speaking from, madam?"

She explained.

"Right. Stay there and we'll have someone with you in ten minutes."

While she waited she took stock. Kenny Cooper was dead, therefore he had not killed the Emersons and run away in a panic, the popular theory to that effect no longer held water. An alternative scenario was needed, so she cast around for one and . . . yes, how about this: Kenny Cooper and X go on a burgling expedition. They are disturbed. X loses his head and attacks the Emersons with the axe. Kenny is hysterical with horror at the sight of so much blood, he is trembling like a jelly and sobbing and ignoring calls to pull himself together. He is a danger to X, he will give the show away unless his mouth is stopped. So X kills him too, then realises that this was quite a clever thing to have done and hides the body. As he had hoped, everyone assumes that moronic

34

delinquent Kenny has murdered the Emersons and run away. End of scenario. But who is X?

One possible answer confronted her on the opposite side of the roundabout: Hodson's Garden Centre, with its entrance brightly lit at night by way of advertisement. It was huge, stretching back from the road over what had once been the gardens and paddocks of a small manor house. It sold everything, from bedding plants and garden string to sit-on mowers and the Venus de Milo in concrete. The owner, Bert Hodson, had worked his way up from a greengrocery stall in a London market, but his route from there to his prosperous garden centre was known to have passed through at least one prison cell and he still operated in the grey area on the edge of the law. There had been a bribery scandal over a planning permission and Celia had twice reported him for the mis-labelling of nursery stock in contravention of the Trade Descriptions Act. This had provoked a visit from Hodson's fat blowsy wife, whose vocabulary of obscene abuse had been an eye-opener. There were also various loutish youths around, allegedly his sons by various women, and one of these was in prison for robbery with violence, or had he been released? She must check the dates. Anyway, Hodson's Garden Centre was a likely hunting ground in the search for X.

The police car which arrived was from the uniformed branch. They were checking on her claim to have unearthed a corpse before they bothered the CID with it.

"Mrs Grant? I'm Sergeant Parsons and this is Constable Robinson. The Towers is right at the top of the village if I remember."

"Yes, but there's a huge tailback up there because of the fire, we'd better go the back way."

Sergeant Parsons nodded. He was one of the new-style policemen, tall and thin like an exclamation mark with a beard. "If you go first we'll follow."

With the police car behind her she threaded her way through narrow winding lanes, past Archerscroft (had Deirdre remembered to shut the cold frames and greenhouse?) and up through the dark avenue of rhododendrons into the stable yard of The Towers.

Sergeant Parsons produced a powerful torch from the boot of the police car. "If you'll just show me the flowerbed in question I needn't keep you. These things are always unpleasant."

She led the way to the lower lawn and pointed. The beam from the torch scanned the area where she had dug. The size of the hole was astonishing. She had no idea she had disturbed so much earth.

Parsons pointed his torch down the hole. "You say you saw a human foot?"

"Yes. There was a shoe but it was rotten. And a sock. I pulled them both off and saw the foot."

Parsons knelt down and rummaged in the hole. "Twilight's very deceptive, isn't it?"

"What d'you mean?"

"Here's the shoe, but I can see nothing down here that resembles a human foot."

"But I saw it quite distinctly. Really. There's no possibility of a mistake."

After more probing he pulled at something which presently came away. "Maybe this is what you mistook for one."

It was a rotten branch from a tree, with the bark bared in patches to show the greyish wood beneath.

"No," said Celia. "I touched his foot. It was soft."

"So's this. Feel. It's all mouldy."

"You don't understand. I took the sock right off to make sure. And there was a frightful smell. There still is."

The odour of death was fainter, but it was still there.

While Parsons went on rummaging around in the hole, Constable Robinson investigated the bushes at the back of the bed. Presently his torch lighted on the corpse of a crow, crawling with maggots.

"Here's what's making the smell," he said disgustedly.

"That wasn't here before. The hole's bigger too. Someone's been here since and taken Kenny Cooper's body away."

There was an ugly pause. Parsons and Constable Robinson exchanged glances which were critical of Celia.

36

"There was a body," she insisted. "It's been taken away."

"Thank you, madam. We needn't trouble you further."

"That was why the haystack was set on fire. To put the phones out of action, so they'd have more time."

"A full investigation will be made in the morning," said Parsons in a voice thick with suppressed bad temper. "I suggest you go indoors now."

Indoors. He meant The Towers. "But I don't live here," she confessed.

Another pause, even heavier with controlled impatience. "You mean, you've been digging up someone else's garden in search of bodies and sending for the police without their knowledge?"

She tried to explain that waiting for Boxie to let her in and coping with Alison when she had the inevitable hysterics would have wasted an enormous amount of time, but Parsons was not listening. "I'll have to call at the house and apologise for intruding," he grumbled.

At all costs this must be prevented. "No, wait," she called as he strode away into the darkness. But it was already too late. The light in the huge mock-Gothic porch was on. Under it stood Alison, beckoning to someone who had just arrived by car; her brother Roy, Nellie's son and Harriet's husband.

It was like a scene from an opera, the despairing heroine sagging at the knees and holding out her arms for succour, the tenor rushing forward to support her, the pair of them clutching each other and staring out from the pool of light into the dark garden. At any moment they would start to sing.

Instead Roy contrived by means of consoling pats and pushes to get Alison back into the house. "What's going on out there?" he shouted.

Roy Armitage was another of the family's genetic mysteries, a little rat-like man with a permanently blue chin. By daylight he was unimpressive, and no one could imagine how he had persuaded the rich, strong-minded Harriet to marry him. Now, dramatically lit from behind, he could be mistaken for a very small toreador. "What the hell's going on?" he repeated.

"I'm sorry sir, there's been an unfortunate misunderstanding," Parsons began.

"Listen Roy, he's got it all wrong," Celia interrupted.

"Just a sec, Celia. Can't listen to two people at once, can I?"

Suddenly she realised that she needed time to think. "Very well, I shall go and sit in my van, and when Sergeant Parsons has given you his version perhaps you'll come and listen to mine."

Who had moved the body? Hunched behind the wheel she tried to decide who besides Nellie knew that she was suspicious about the herbaceous border and intended to dig it up. Alison presumably, Nellie must have told her. Nigel. He had taken the trouble to stroll over from his flat in the stables and find out what she was doing. Deirdre. She would have mentioned it to her sulky lump of a Timothy when she got home. Ron's mother was a notorious gossip, the whole council estate would have known within half an hour. One of the loutish Hodson youths had fathered a child and married the girl, they lived two doors from Ron. From there the news would have spread quickly to the garden centre. Among all these people there was someone who had taken alarm because he knew what Celia would find when she dug.

Celia put herself in X's place. What was he to do, don a stocking mask, knock her unconscious before she began to dig, and whisk the corpse away? That would merely prove that her widely publicised suspicions were correct. How much subtler to let her make her gruesome discovery, then remove Kenny while she was fetching the police. It would be easy to discredit her story, destroy her credibility. A woman of that age, the change, you know. They tend to imagine things.

But X must have asked himself how long it would take her to fetch the police. Long enough for him to remove an already half-excavated body? It would be safer to put a few obstacles in her way. Cut a few telephone wires, perhaps? No, a deliberately cut phone wire would be proof that something was wrong, almost as bad as hitting her over the head. A match applied to a strategically placed haystack, then. Much better.

38

Who knew which way the lines came into the village? Everyone with a telephone unfortunately. Attention was drawn to this matter in every winter storm, when broken branches brought down the lines and cut the village off.

"Now, Celia." Roy's ferocious bark in her ear made her jump. He was glaring in at her angrily through the van window, with his rat-like teeth bared under the wispy moustache. "Been making a damn fool of yourself, I hear,"

"Listen, Roy, there *was* a body, I pulled off the shoe and the sock and . . ."

"How dare you put a scare like that into Alison with your comic capers? Marching in here and digging up flowerbeds without so much as a by your leave."

"I asked your mother's permission. She owns this place."

"Who said you could call the police?"

"Alison would have had hysterics if I'd asked her. I looked for Nigel but he was out."

"Damn it, Celia, you know as well as I do, Alison's been on the brink for years, nearly went over the edge when someone decided to use Wheelwright's as a damn slaughterhouse. And now all this about a corpse that isn't there, are you trying to shoo her into a loony-bin or what?"

"Listen, Roy. There *was* a body . . ."

"If she goes into a bin she'll be there for keeps, and it'll be your fault and I shall personally make it my business to see that you suffer for it."

This infuriated Celia. "If Alison has a nervous breakdown it'll be because you and Harriet have never done a hand's turn to help her cope with a very demanding old lady who treats her like a doormat because Alison's too meek to stand up to her."

He reached into the car and gripped her wrist. "What the hell business is that of yours?"

"Please let go of my arm, Roy, I begin to wonder if you are sane. That's better. Now pull yourself together. Try to grasp that the world is a wicked place and that unpleasant things such as murders and the discovery of bodies are not going to refrain from

39

happening for fear of putting you and your wife to the inconvenience of having to look after your mother. There was a body there, I saw it quite distinctly, but you're in no state to discuss the thing rationally, and I think we'd better talk in the morning. Good night."

She shot off down the drive, still trembling with anger. As the rhododendrons flashed past on either side her headlights picked out a figure standing motionless on the verge. She stopped. It was Nigel.

"The police have just come roaring by," he said. "Do I gather that there was a body after all?"

"Yes."

"How interesting. Whose?"

"Kenny Cooper's, I assume. He's the only missing person."

"That will put the cat among the pigeons," said Nigel. "He was popular as a murder suspect but he raises awkward questions as a corpse."

"I imagine it was him, but I only excavated his foot."

"They can check at the autopsy, teeth are very revealing."

"There won't be an autopsy," said Celia. "While I was getting the police someone grubbed him up and took him away."

Nigel savoured this silently. "I say, what fun."

"Not for me. I shall be widely accused of having menopausal delusions."

"Isn't it a bit early for your menopause?"

"Yes. You didn't notice unusual activity in the garden after I left?"

"No, I'd gone out to eat."

He always ate in the pub, she remembered. Too lazy to cook.

"Anyone could have come in from Butler's Copse, though," he went on, "without being seen from the house."

"Someone in the wood could have been watching me dig."

"Yes. And waiting to whisk Kenny away the moment you went for the police."

There was a silence. She reached for the ignition key, but Nigel stopped her with a gesture. He had something more to say. "I

40

suppose this reopens the whole question of the Emersons, etc. As you probably know, Dame Rumour has been busy with my name in that connection."

"No?"

"The suggestion is that I wielded the fatal axe and have somehow managed to shove the onus off on Kenny."

"Most of the onus-shoving has been done by your Aunt Harriet and friends. They've been behaving like town criers on the subject. Everyone thinks they're protecting someone, but I hadn't gathered it was you."

"Yes, I wish they wouldn't because it's quite unnecessary. Just in case you get any ideas I thought I'd just mention that I have an alibi for the Emersons' murder and also I suppose for Kenny Cooper's murder if you're right and he has been murdered. If you ask the police they'll tell you that according to four independent witnesses I was busy at the relevant time, in accordance with my daily custom, eating fried plaice and chips and peas or something of that sort in the saloon bar of the Westfield Arms."

He paused again. The secretive smile was in place, but he was watching her shrewdly. "Is Uncle Roy here?"

"I think he's with your mother."

"In that case I must go and give her moral support, he terrifies her."

"Everything terrifies her," said Celia. "The burglar alarm's on in the daytime now, it's dreadful. D'you know what she's really afraid of?"

"No . . . I wish I did. Goodnight."

FOUR

CELIA SLEPT LATE and woke wondering why her misery-quotient was so high. The phone was ringing. It was Timothy Foster, Deirdre's husband. He had a dark comfortable voice and sounded much nicer on the telephone than he was.

"Bad news, I'm afraid. Deirdre's mother's had a fall, she's had to rush off to look after her."

"Oh. I'm sorry."

"Yes, it's a broken femur unfortunately. Deirdre asked me to say she's sorry, but she doesn't know when she'll be able to get back. Can you manage without her for a bit?"

"Oh, I expect so," said Celia as cheerfully as she could, but this was disastrous. She was now short of her only competent assistant and one of her motor mowers at the height of the busy spring season. "Say I hope her mother makes a good recovery," she told Timothy, "and she's not to worry."

There was a pause, during which she remembered her reason for feeling miserable.

"I say, Celia. I was sorry to hear about last night."

Celia hesitated. "I'm not sure what you mean."

"The false alarm at The Towers."

"Ah. It remains to be seen if the alarm was false or not."

"Well . . . twilight's very deceptive, isn't it?"

"Who told you, Timothy?"

"I dropped in at the pub for a nightcap. It seemed to be common knowledge."

When the call was over she was pleased with the way she had handled it. It was disagreeable news that she had already become the talk of the Westfield Arms as a hysterical goose who had called the police to examine a non-existent corpse, and it was even possible that Deirdre had invented her mother's leg as an excuse to dissociate herself from her ridiculed employer. But she had managed to sound calm. That had been an instinctive reaction but she saw now that she must, as a conscious policy, exhibit vast quantities of poise. She would practise fixing her face in a dignified mask like the Queen, who never looked put out whatever happened. From now on the village must see her as a common-sensical lady who dealt cheerfully with every difficulty and never showed dismay.

It was Saturday morning and the frame yard was soon full of customers. Coping with them all without Deirdre was difficult, but she forced herself not to run or look harassed and even managed to put her policy into effect when the purchaser of twelve *Iris unguicularis* "Mary Barnard" revealed that he proposed to plant them along the damp margin of his lily-pool. But her attempt at serene poise was disrupted by the arrival of a police car containing Sergeant Parsons, looking self-important. This caused a stir among the customers and a buzz of talk, so she hurried him into her little office just inside the back door. By daylight the beard no longer disguised the fact that he was very young.

"Now Mrs Grant," he began. "The CID made a thorough investigation of that flowerbed this morning. There are no human remains in it, and no evidence that any human remains were ever there."

"But . . ."

He held up a hand. "I'll just finish if I may. I'm quite satisfied that you *thought* you saw the foot of a corpse there. I have no intention of starting proceedings for causing a public mischief and wasting police time. In saying that I take into account that you have been under stress, but in future I hope you'll leave detection to the police. If there had been a body in the garden at The Towers, your interference would have destroyed valuable evidence."

Celia put on her polite mask and wondered what would happen if she hit him with the rolled-up seed catalogue she was gripping in the effort to keep her temper.

43

"Thank you so much for telling me," she said sweetly. "May I ask you one or two questions?"

"Certainly, Mrs Grant."

"As you know, I'm a professional gardener and maintain gardens under contract, including the one at The Towers. Are you forbidding me to dig in case I unearth something which might be of police interest?"

"Of course not, where there are no suspicious circumstances."

"Good. Now let's decide what circumstances are suspicious. You seem to be suggesting that next time a patch of perennials in a border doesn't come up and I don't understand why, I shouldn't investigate myself but ring for the CID."

"I'm sure you understand what I meant, Mrs Grant."

"I don't, but never mind. You also said you 'knew I'd been under stress'. I wonder what you meant by that?"

Parsons shifted uncomfortably in his chair. Celia kept up her mask of polite enquiry and decided that if he so much as hinted at the menopause, she would stuff the seed catalogue down his throat.

"No doubt your remark was based on 'information received'," she went on, "after making character enquiries about me in the village."

"I'm not at liberty to discuss that."

"Of course not, you have to protect your sources. But if you've been listening to gossip surely I'm entitled to comment on what you've been told?"

"As to that . . . discussing it would serve no useful purpose."

"Really? I wonder why not?"

"It would . . . embarrass you," he said, as areas not covered by beard began to go very red.

"Oh no, I don't think so. When you said you knew I'd been under stress, you must have had some particular form of stress in mind. I'm entitled to know what it is."

Parsons looked at her unhappily, like a dog in disgrace. "I . . . was thinking of Mrs Foster going off and leaving you short-handed."

44

"But I only heard about that this morning when her husband rang. How can I have been under stress last night because of something I didn't know about till this morning?"

"You knew beforehand, though, that she was leaving."

"Leaving? You mean for good? Is that what you've been told?"

"Yes. You must have known she would after the er, disagreement," said Parsons on a rising note of panic.

"What disagreement?"

She repeated the question several times without getting a reply.

"Oh gawd," said Parsons. Veins were standing out on his scarlet forehead in great knots.

"Oh!" cried Celia as light dawned. "Oh you poor young man, don't worry, it's always happening, you'll learn as you grow older. Whenever two women set up together in business, someone's going to start a rumour that they're lesbians . . ."

His jaw had dropped, leaving a round 'o' of mouth in the middle of the beard; a sight which sent her off into helpless giggles.

"I'm sorry but . . . your face," she spluttered. "Deirdre and I are supposed to have had a lovers' tiff, is that it?"

Laughing had been a mistake. He was very, very angry. "Nothing of the sort. Mrs Foster's a married woman," he snapped.

The implications of this remark took a few moments to sink in. When they did Celia was very angry too. "Oh. I see now. I'm supposed to be gay and I made a pass at Deirdre Foster who's straight, and she was shocked and disgusted and will have nothing more to do with me. Is that what you've been told?"

"I prefer not to discuss it."

"Now listen to me, young man. I'm not good at spotting lesbians and you couldn't tell one from the back axle of a police car, so get this into your head. I am *not* gay, I parted with Deirdre Foster last night on normal friendly terms, I am perfectly sane and not under stress, and you ought to look very carefully at the motives of whoever fed you this nonsense; because I *did* unearth the foot of a corpse, and it's not my fault if it wasn't there when I came back with you."

The bearded mouth bared its teeth in a sneer. "Having been taken away by beings from outer space, no doubt."

Naughty naughty, thought Celia, I shall punish you for that. "I beg your pardon? I don't understand."

"I think my meaning was obvious."

"Not to me. You said something about beings from outer space. Surely you don't believe in them? Or was it intended as a joke?" She counted ten slowly. "Oh dear. I believe it was."

"Nobody removed a body, there wasn't time," Parsons snapped.

"Are you sure? I can think of five people who knew by half past four that I'd noticed something odd about the planting in that border and intended to dig it up. Between them they could have told dozens of others. Anyone who knew Kenny Cooper's body was there would have had hours to lay his plans. He could watch me from Butler's Copse and move in to start unearthing Kenny the moment I left to fetch the police."

"Knowing you might be back in a few minutes."

"On the contrary. Knowing that all the telephones in the village had been put out of action."

"There is no evidence that the haystack fire at Barton's Farm was deliberately caused, or that if deliberately caused, it was connected with events at The Towers."

Celia stood up. "There is no firm evidence of a connection between the rise in violent crime and violence on television. But you and I know perfectly well that they're very closely connected indeed. Good morning, Sergeant Parsons."

When he had gone she sat in her office for a moment, breathing heavily and getting her woe-coefficient under control. Someone was spreading stories about her, first at the Westfield Arms and now this nonsense about her and Deirdre which had been fed to the police to destroy her credibility. Presently she would try to think who this someone could be, but the frame yard was full of customers agog with curiosity. She switched on her dignified mask and went out to face them.

She worked flat out till closing time, then drove into the village,

46

where she had a duty to perform. The shop was already shut for the night. Quaking inwardly she rang the bell at the side door leading to the living quarters. After what had happened Ethel Cooper might slam it in her face, but to stay away would be unforgiveable.

"I was afraid all along of something like this," said Ethel sadly, pouring out sticky brown sherry for herself and Celia. "Kenny was fond of me, he'd never have gone so long without getting in touch."

"You've only got my word for it though," Celia reminded her. "The police say I'm half-mad and there never was a body there."

"Course there was, dear, and it was took away while you was phoning. Haystacks don't set fire to themselves, do they? Trust the police to get it wrong."

This was her cue for a long tirade against the constabulary. They had maliciously persecuted her Kenny, who was a good boy at heart and only went wrong because they'd given him a bad name. They were lazy, and saved themselves trouble by blaming Kenny for all the petty crime for miles around. Of course Kenny had gone to the bad when he knew he was going to get the blame anyway.

"D'you think Kenny was at Wheelwright's that night?"

"Must have been dear, else he'd still be alive. I know what happened, I worked it all out. It was that nasty Nigel Fitzgerald up at The Towers. He's broke 'cos them silly sculptures of his don't sell, so he gets my Kenny to help him and they burgled the place together and the Emersons disturbed them. Well, Fitzgerald was gentry and he'd a lot to lose, so he killed them. Now my Kenny, he's not cruel, he can't bear to see an animal suffer even. He tried to stop him laying into the Emersons with that axe, so Fitzgerald killed him too."

It was Celia's own scenario, with Nigel Fitzgerald miscast in the role of X.

"I knew that was it," Ethel swept on, "soon as they said at the inquest about the blood in the wood."

According to the forensic evidence drops of blood, of a different group from the Emersons, had been traced in a trail leading into Butler's Copse, where they petered out. According to Ethel's theory, Kenny had run away wounded into the wood, where Nigel had finished him off.

There was at least one thing wrong with this version of the drama. "Ethel dear, it couldn't have been Nigel. He wasn't there."

"Who says?"

"The times don't fit. Don't you remember, the police came round asking everyone where they'd been between eight and nine that night, because that was the important time? Nigel says that according to four witnesses he was eating his dinner in the Westfield Arms when the Emersons were killed."

"The police told me that, and I told them Fitzgerald and his witnesses was bloody liars. They was all saloon bar regulars, cronies of his. Course they backed him up."

"But Ethel, if he'd committed a murder, would he ask people to fake an alibi for him? He wouldn't dare, sooner or later it would come out."

Ethel shook her head obstinately. "Then the police got the time of the murder wrong."

This too seemed unlikely. According to the evidence at the inquest Mrs Emerson's watch had been smashed as she tried to protect her head. It had stopped at eight thirty or thereabouts.

"All I know is, Kenny was out with Fitzgerald that night," Ethel insisted.

"Oh? I didn't realise they even knew each other. I've never seen them going about together."

"Oh no dear, that was Fitzgerald's cunning. Kenny never let on, but they knew each other all right."

"Are you sure?"

Ethel nodded. "Kenny never said, there was lots he never told me, but I knew. Fitzgerald got Kenny to help him with them nasty pranks of his, putting dummies in the road at the roundabout and so on."

Surprisingly this was believable. Nigel went in for elaborate practical jokes which he probably thought of as "happenings" and extensions of his sculpture, and which often seemed to require the help of an accomplice. He was widely suspected of having organised the appearance of a sow whose litter was expected hourly at the wedding reception of the village's most pregnant bride, and had almost certainly staged a realistic road accident, consisting of four tailor's dummies and much tomato sauce, which had caused chaos at the roundabout near Hodson's Garden Centre. At the hunt point-to-point he had persuaded a small crowd to walk round and round a water-tower with no entrance following arrows that said "Toilet". But he always managed to cover his tracks. When skids in the tomato sauce at the roundabout prompted police enquiries he had produced a fairly convincing alibi.

"There was things one person couldn't do alone," Ethel argued. "Remember the Blossom Route notices?"

Every spring the motoring organisations signposted a "Blossom Route" through miles of fruit orchards in flower. For most of an Easter weekend a procession of cars in search of blossom had been diverted through a depressing panorama of sewage beds, battery chicken houses and carbreakers' yards into the muddy car park of an evil-smelling glue factory.

"Ethel, are you quite sure Nigel Fitzgerald got Kenny to help him? How d'you know if Kenny didn't say?"

"Easy. It always happened the same, on a Friday night mostly. There'd be the phone call: 'Can I speak to Kenny', in a funny voice, not like his other friends, it was someone not speaking natural. I'd know what it was because Kenny wouldn't put on his fancy clothes for fear of spoiling them, and another thing, those times he never took his moped. I suppose he walked to The Towers or Fitzgerald picked him up in a car. Anyway, he'd go out all excited, like when he was going to a party. Then he'd come back late, I always waited up for him, and he'd have what I called his silly-clever look and he'd be smelling of whisky and confused like, and I'd know we'd hear about one of that Fitzgerald's nasty pranks in the morning."

"Was he out with Fitzgerald the night the Emersons were killed?"

"Yes."

Somehow this "yes" did not have the ring of certainty.

"He rang up then?" Celia said. "Asking in a funny voice to speak to Kenny?"

"Only after I went out. I'd slipped out to the Women's Institute see, it was one of their evenings, and Kenny was sitting in here polishing his boots that I gave him for Christmas that he was so proud of, and that was the last I set eyes on him. When I went off to the Institute."

After a tearful pause she went on. "When I got back he wasn't here. He hadn't changed into his best gear and his moped was there so I said to myself, that Fitzgerald must have phoned and he's gone out. Well, I waited up as usual but he never came and in the end I went to bed but I never closed my eyes and in the morning he still wasn't there, but his moped was still in the shed. That was the worst thing. All this time I've been saying to people how he'd run away because he was afraid of being blamed. But I kept asking myself, if he's run away, why didn't he do it on his moped?"

The tears came now in a flood. Celia gave what comfort she could, but wondered at the same time how much of all this to believe. Nigel seemed an unlikely partner for Kenny on a housebreaking expedition, and the evidence of a connection between the two of them was very thin. The only hard fact seemed to be that Kenny had gone out on a mysterious expedition on various occasions when Nigel was mounting one of his practical jokes. That could easily be a coincidence, and it soon became clear from Ethel's answers that all Kenny's evening expeditions were mysterious. What other friends did he have? What cafes or amusement arcades did he frequent? She did not know. On most evenings he simply disappeared on his moped without telling her where he was going. Her only solid information was a list of unskilled jobs he had walked out of or lost.

"D'you think he knew the Hodson boys, Ethel? Two of them have police records and the whole set-up's pretty shady."

The Hodson boys seemed far more likely starters as house-breaking companions for Kenny, but Ethel did not know.

"If Kenny was looking for bad company to lead him astray," Celia persisted, "there's plenty of it in that garden centre. The father has a prison record and so has one of the boys at least. The police are always there."

"I know dear, Florence Clay's eldest girl works on the checkout. She says there's funny goings-on."

"Too right there are. The stock's mostly overpriced rubbish and they don't care what they put on the labels."

"That's not what I meant, dear. Something queer. There's a shed no one's allowed in, and every day about noon a big van arrives and drives in and they shut the doors before they unload it. She thinks there's meetings or something going on in there, people coming in and staying a long time."

"Goodness, what sort of people?"

"Commercial travellers. That sort."

Celia thought about this. "Quite a few village people work in the garden centre, don't they? Could you try to find out a bit more? Casually? I can't, the village will laugh its head off if there's any more brilliant detective work by me."

"No dear, we won't. If you say you saw Kenny's foot that's good enough for us. You don't realise, we're all very fond of you. We none of us believe that nonsense."

"About me and Deirdre Foster?" said Celia. Too late, she realised that she had misunderstood.

Ethel had gone scarlet. "I meant the nonsense the police say. But I'd heard the other too."

"D'you know who started it?"

"No dear, I wish I did. Trying to make out you're a bad woman, so you won't be believed. It's the same people, the ones that are saying I know where Kenny is."

"Ethel, try to find out who it is. If we knew that we could make sense of the whole thing."

"Find out who started a rumour?" Ethel laughed bitterly. "In *this* village?"

51

FIVE

WHEN CELIA WAS short-handed her only hope of staying sane was to get as many routine jobs as possible done during the weekend. On Sunday morning she was pricking out seedlings of her *corsicus niger* hellebore when a loutish young man she had seen somewhere before pushed open the gate from the lane. He looked like a gipsy and his shirt was wide open to exhibit a formidable mat of black hair.

"Sorry, we're shut on Sundays," said Celia. "Did I forget to put the notice on the gate?"

"Thass okay," said the youth. "Me dad wassa word with you."

A big dirty car swept into the yard and Bert Hodson, the owner of the infamous garden centre, got out from behind the wheel.

"Morning, Miz Grant, nice day. You thought any more about that offer o'mine?"

"Let me see, what offer was that?"

"Concentrate dear, you remember. Sixty thousand for the cottage and land and goodwill of the business."

"I told you months ago I wasn't interested," said Celia.

"But don't you want to have another think, after that dreadful embarrassing experience of yours on Friday night? Made a right patsy of yourself, didn't you?"

"What experience of mine was embarrassing, Mr Hodson?"

"Seeing a body that wasn't there, and putting the police to all that inconvenience." He turned to the loutish young man. "Me heart bleeds for the pore lady, doesn't yours Jim?"

Jim nodded solemnly. "That's right."

"So why don't you have another think, dearie?" said Hodson. "You'd be better off away from here."

Ignoring this, Celia studied him. "You puzzle me, Mr Hodson. We're not in competition, this is a specialist nursery dealing in small quantities of stock that wouldn't interest you. Why d'you want to buy me out?"

"There's personal reasons," he said, leering.

"You mean, because you'd labelled six dozen scruffy little *bealei* as *Mahonia* 'Charity'? And I shopped you?"

"That was very spiteful of you, dear. Anyone can make a mistake."

"People who make as many 'mistakes' as you do should be made to sell second-hand cars, so the customers know you're dishonest."

"Oh deary me Jim, she will have her little joke."

"Why d'you want to buy me out?" Celia persisted.

"I've took a fancy to this desirable cottage residence," said Hodson playfully. "Always wanted to live in a cottage."

"It's not nearly grand enough for you, far too few gold taps. Tell me the real reason."

Father and son looked at each other and sniggered, then wandered off down the line of cold frames casting a supercilious eye over her stock. At the frame containing her double primroses, three more of which were now showing colour, they stopped and struck dramatic attitudes of admiration.

"Oh Jim, look at them lovely double primroses, we ought to stock those." He turned to Celia. "Give you a pound a dozen for them."

"Sorry. They're not for sale."

"Ah. Rarities are they dear? Some special cross you've bred up yourself? There's a lot of money in rarities, they say, if they don't get pinched off of you. I've often thought, Jim, we should take out plant breeders' rights on something, make a fortune. We must remember them lovely primroses."

"Look, I'm very busy," said Celia. "And I've answered your question. The nursery is not for sale, nor is it open for business on Sundays, so will you please go."

53

Hodson made a great parade of losing patience with her. "Come on, Jim, we're off. Waste of time talking to her, pore thing, she won't listen to good advice. She'll not enjoy staying here, after what happened. People looking at her and whispering."

"Thass right dad."

"And this little cottage of hers is so isolated. Easy to break into, too." Hodson climbed back into his car. "In her place I'd not risk it, eh Jim? I'd get out now."

Should she get out, Celia wondered when they had gone. When Hodson first made his offer she had turned it down flat, but now she was tempted. She could sell at a fat profit and start again in some village less full of snake venom than Westfield. With the extra capital she could probably manage without the chore of the garden maintenance contracts. But sell to Hodson? Slink away, leaving Westfield to conclude that she knew she had made a fool of herself and could not face the ridicule? No.

She weeded and pricked out grimly for the rest of the morning, then ate a hasty bread and cheese lunch and, cursing slightly, went upstairs to deal with her appearance. This was the Sunday when the Old Rectory garden was open to the public in aid of cancer research. Everyone would be there. She would go, parading her new unruffled calm, and she was damned if she would run the gauntlet of village curiosity looking like a frump.

Presently she studied herself in the long mirror. The coat and skirt, a survivor from her grand London days, still fitted and the cut was casual enough not to look too dressed up. She had bought it to go to the Palace for Roger's OBE, but the soft pink was even more of a knockout now that her hair was silver-grey.

The Old Rectory belonged to Roy and Harriet Armitage. In the past few days she had exchanged heavy artillery fire with both of them, but that was no reason for staying away. Village etiquette decreed that factional strife must not interfere with social intercourse or support for good causes. Sworn enemies were allowed to chat amicably at charity events and also in private houses on occasions where gin was served, so it was perfectly proper for Celia to enter the Old Rectory garden under a flag of truce. Indeed failure to contribute her pound to cancer research would have earned her a black mark. Roy would probably be looking after car parking in the paddock as usual, and in accordance with village custom they would exchange a few civilised words as if nothing had happened. The same convention would apply in theory when she went inside and confronted Harriet, but with less certainty that the exchange would be civilised. Harriet believed firmly in the right of the rich to be rude.

Surprisingly there was no sign of Roy in the paddock. The parking was being supervised by the gardener, helped by the youngest Armitage boy. Steeling herself, she paid her pound at the wicket gate and went in, ignoring curious glances and paying attention to her horticultural surroundings. Harriet's garden was too small to be so grand. The Rhododendron Dell, the Alpine Garden, the Old Rose Walk and the Lily Pool Court with its twin gazebos had been tarted up as if for inspection by royalty, but fewer of these features treated more spaciously would have produced a more restful effect.

When she emerged on to the crowded South Lawn people stopped talking and stared at her with gloomy hostility, like cows inspecting an intruder into their field. She was a class traitor, she had dared to cast doubt on the obvious fact that the Emersons had been killed by a Person Unlike Us. Harriet Armitage, who was holding court in the middle of the lawn, greeted her arrival as a grave social crisis. Her eyes bulged with effort as she searched for something harmless to say. "Ah, Celia. The Wild Garden has been quite inadequate this spring, I was right and you were wrong. Not nearly enough hepaticas."

Hepaticas, which grew wild all over central and northern Europe, were obtainable in England only with difficulty and expense. Celia had sold Harriet all she could lay hands on at a hefty profit.

"I wanted great drifts," Harriet complained.

"I told you, they often don't flower the first year. You should have bought great drifts of the blue *Anemone blanda* from a supermarket, much cheaper and less trouble."

"But everyone has *Anemone blanda*, even that vulgar public park at Sissinghurst. Hepaticas are much nicer."

The whole scene had come to a standstill. Everyone was staring and trying to catch what they were saying.

Harriet collected her wits and decided sensibly that Celia must be fed an exit line. "Now, Celia. We're short-handed, my tiresome Roy's gone off to Yorkshire or somewhere to look at a horse, so I'm appointing you policeman. Off you go—and keep a sharp look out. The finger blight* last year was appalling."

Harriet was obsessed with the idea that her garden would be stripped by pilferers whenever she opened it. Celia promised to be vigilant, though the number of plants at risk was quite small. Exploring, she found that the purple border and the orange border were still showing very little colour, but thanks to a froth of *Clematis montana* and a heavy expenditure on tulips the White Garden was already able to make the point that it was white. The roses which would take over this task in June were not Iceberg, the obvious choice. Determined to avoid the commonplace, Harriet had ransacked Europe for supplies of a long-forgotten white hybrid perpetual called Frau Karl Drushki.

But surely there was some mistake? Not all the roses were Frau Karl Drushki, or even hybrid perpetuals. Someone had interplanted them with what looked like a job lot of miscellaneous roses from an inferior garden centre. And on the wire arch, which led through to the Blue Garden beyond, someone had trained up the shoots of a thornless climbing rose which she recognised at once. The untruthful label read "Sanders White".

While making these discoveries she had been carefully ignoring a man who was standing near her. It turned out to be Nigel, wearing his usual secret smile. "I was afraid you'd spot it," he murmured, fingering the smooth shoots of the climbing rose. "Don't give the show away, will you?"

*This condition, to which geraniums are especially prone, is found after gardens have been open to the public and is caused by the surreptitious removal by visitors of shoots to be struck as cuttings. The plant is often reduced to a skeleton, or in severe cases disappears completely.

56

So this was one of Nigel's practical jokes.

"What are they?" she asked, nodding towards the scruffy invaders in the white rose beds.

"Mostly Frensham and Masquerade and one of those corpse-like lavender-grey affairs, I forget its name."

Frensham was a dismal red floribunda and a martyr to mildew. Masquerade was a fierce red and yellow bicolour and the thornless climber on the arch was of course Zephirine Drouhin, a violent pink job guaranteed to wreck any colour scheme it got involved in. The White Garden would look hellish when all this burst into bloom.

"Promise you won't tell Aunt Harriet," Nigel whispered.

"She'll notice."

"No. She's very unobservant."

"Simpson will," Celia objected. Simpson was Harriet's gardener.

Nigel grinned. "Simpson's strictly a dahlia and vegetable marrow man, he doesn't hold with her highfaluting ideas."

"Does he know?"

"He planted them for me."

So Nigel had bribed Simpson. It would be easy, he loathed Harriet and only stayed because she cringed and offered him yet more money every time he was rude to her and threatened to leave.

"This garden's an obscenity, I had to make a gesture," said Nigel. "Promise not to tell?"

"I'll think about it," said Celia, and walked on into the Blue Garden, where the Isaacsons and the Spencers were chatting loudly by a sundial. They fell silent when they saw her. She gave them a cool good afternoon and walked on through an archway leading back to the South Lawn. Behind her Mary Spencer hissed, "Oh my God, d'you think she heard?"

Out on the lawn a farm labourer's wife gave her a sweet smile and she stopped to chat. Two more families from the village joined her, then a third, in a discreet demonstration of support. Presently bull-like glares from Harriet made it clear that she was not having anyone set up a rival court on her lawn.

"Don't you take no notice of her," said a little old lady whose name Celia could not remember. "You stick to your guns dear, and watch out for that Fitzgerald at The Towers, he's behind all this."

"Actually, he's got an alibi for the Emersons' murder," Celia objected.

"Haystacks don't set fire to themselves, dear, not at this time of year."

Celia decided that this subversive gathering had better end before Harriet lowered her head and charged across the grass to break it up. Moving on into the crowd she found herself avoiding Bert Hodson and his enormous red-haired wife, a shapeless cascade of flesh in dirty purple satin.

"There is the pore lady now," he said loudly, "the one I told you about dear. Such a pity, she'd be better off out of the village."

Celia went up to him. "Now now, Mr Hodson, we're all here to enjoy ourselves, so don't be a spoilsport. Nobody's making snide remarks about garden centres that break the Trade Descriptions Act, so just you shut up about me."

She smiled round at the goggling onlookers and withdrew, wondering if she had done the right thing. To be silent was to cringe, but was a sharp retort evidence of jagged nerves? There was no way one could win. Worrying about this she failed to look where she was going and ran slap into the podgy chest and stomach of Timothy Foster, Deirdre's husband.

Timothy's damp hands held on to her longer than was necessary to help her back on to her balance. "Hullo there," he said in his over-rich baritone. "Bearing up, I hope, despite everything?"

"Yes thank you. It's a nuisance being without Deirdre, but I expect I'll manage."

He was still holding her elbow and his watery brown eyes were full of concern. "Oh good. But I wasn't really thinking of that."

"Then I don't know what you were thinking of," she said crisply, freeing herself. "But I'd like Deirdre's phone number. There are some loose ends I need to ask her about."

"Oh." To her surprise he began to go pink. "She's . . . with her mother."

"I know. In Sussex, isn't it?"

"No, her mother was staying with friends in Hampshire when it happened and got taken to the hospital there. There's some talk of moving her back to Brighton, but to be honest I don't know how to get hold of Deirdre at the moment."

He was so red that he had to be lying. What was all this? Had he invented Deirdre's mother's broken leg and whisked her away because he thought she needed protection from Celia's lesbian advances? If so, why was he patting Celia's hand so tenderly? He was sweating a little and the eyes in his fat face were urgent with emotion, he looked like a randy sea-lion.

"I know you're having a difficult time just now," he murmured, massaging her left arm. "If there's anything I can do don't hesitate, give me a ring, any time, and I'll be round."

These approaches were no surprise to Celia. She had sensed for some time that he would have a behaviour problem the moment Deirdre's back was turned, as it so mysteriously was now. But his protective urge seemed ill-timed, unless he thought a woman who had made a fool of herself and needed comfort would be easy meat.

"Remember, if there's anything I can do . . ."

"There is, actually," said Celia, remembering that he was a partner in a firm of estate agents. "You can tell me why someone's offering to buy Archerscroft from me for sixty thousand when it's only worth forty-five at most."

"Who is?"

"Bert Hodson. And he more or less says he'll rough me up rotten if I refuse to sell."

Timothy's protective ardour suddenly evaporated. Evidently "anything I can do" did not include protecting her against the Hodson family's displeasure.

"Oh, I don't think he meant it, Celia. I know him quite well, his bark's worse than his bite."

"Seriously though, why does he want it?"

He seemed to have no ideas about this, so Celia expounded a theory she had worked out for herself. The land behind the garden

59

centre, consisting of coppice woodland and a few meadows let out for rough grazing, belonging to a local solicitor. If Hodson wanted to expand his garden centre the obvious course was to buy this not very valuable land. Moreover it backed on to the bottom of Celia's garden.

"So if he bought Archerscroft from me as well," she concluded, "he'd have another way in and out *via* the back lane, which I suppose would be a convenience. But could he get planning permission?"

"No. The lane's too narrow for commercial vehicles, the police would object on traffic grounds."

"I imagine Bert Hodson usually fixes that sort of thing with a fistful of twenty pound notes."

"Oh come," said Timothy primly. "You mustn't believe everything you hear."

Celia gave him up as hopeless. He was hollow, like a silly fat balloon. There was nothing to be got out of him but hot air—it would rush out with a hiss if one pricked him. Why could he not discuss the Hodson problem frankly? What was all this mystery about Deirdre?

"Anyway tell Deirdre I want a word with her if she rings you," she said and left him abruptly.

As she crossed the lawn a deputation consisting of Lucinda Fox-Norton and Harriet blocked her way.

"Minx," said Lucinda.

"Celia, you have made a disgusting exhibition of yourself," said Harriet.

Celia was amazed. "Why am I a disgusting exhibition?"

"Flinging yourself at that unfortunate man's head," said Harriet.

"Whose? You can't mean Timothy Foster? Oh no, Harriet, any flinging that went on was in the opposite direction."

"I'd have thought you were in enough trouble already without misbehaving in public," said Harriet and swept on with her nose in the air.

Celia escaped into the Wild Garden to pull herself together and

60

start looking calm again. It was a spring garden and the main display was over, leaving nothing much to see. At first there was no one about, but after a few minutes she was reminded sharply that she was supposed to be on the lookout for light-fingered visitors. One recognised the signs with practice, the slightly too casual walk, the slow calm turning of the head to see if anyone was looking, the handbag or whatever at the ready to receive the booty. On all three counts the woman in a fur coat who had just entered the Wild Garden by another path was about to steal.

She was not very good at it. Her glance round before she stooped down was obviously furtive and she ought to have spotted that Celia, though pretending not to notice, had a clear view of what she was doing, namely scratching something up with bare but beringed hands. Not a hepatica, something bigger. A cyclamen, one of the spring-flowering *repandums*. Celia had a clear view of the marbled leaf as it was pushed into the expensive leather handbag.

She wondered what to do. She foresaw unpleasantness and was in no mood to do Harriet a favour. But stealing was stealing, she herself had lost one of her hellebores to pilferers, one of the prize-winning *corsicus* hybrids that she had a three-year waiting list of customers for. She owed it to a fellow-gardener to take action, and it would be only prudent to seize a chance of mending her fences with Harriet.

There was a drill on these occasions. The culprit must never be tackled until a witness was available. Celia followed her back to the South Lawn where Harriet was still holding court, and told her what she had seen.

The unpleasantest part of the business was that Harriet enjoyed it. "Show me," she said eagerly. "Where?"

The fur-coated woman was wandering towards the exit. Harriet charged up to her wearing her fiercest startled-bullock glare. "Would you please come into the house for a moment?"

"Why, pliss?" The accent was vaguely central European.

"It will be less embarrassing in the house."

"Embarrasink, what is embarrassink?" said the woman loudly. "I don't understand you."

"I believe you have something in your handbag which does not belong to you. A plant."

"You are accusink me of stealink?" she cried, so loudly that people turned to look. Celia was puzzled. Pilferers caught red-handed were often indignant, as if helping oneself to other people's plants was not stealing but a perfectly proper thing to do. After a bit of bluster they usually let themselves be taken aside while the thing was dealt with, but this woman was deliberately building up a scene for a whole lawnful of people to witness. She was a woman of the utmost respectability, she said, the insult was unheard-of, her lawyers would sue Harriet, the damages would be enormous.

"We can settle this very easily," said Harriet, "if you will let me look in your handbag."

In the split second while the handbag was being passed to Harriet, Celia knew that she had fallen into a trap. There would be no cyclamen in it, the woman had jettisoned it somewhere. This was a ploy to establish in front of the whole village that Celia suffered from delusions and had seen no corpse in the garden of The Towers.

"Celia, there is no plant in here," said Harriet in a shocked voice.

There was a long silence.

"My pockets, I insist that you are searchink my pockets," cried the woman, taking off her fur coat. There was nothing in them either.

"There has been a mistake," said Harriet majestically. "I offer you my humblest apologies."

"I am not blamink you, it is her fault," the woman cried, rounding on Celia. "You will make me apology and pay me big damages."

"Then you'd better give me your name and address," Celia suggested.

"No, I will not."

"If you're going to sue me for damages I'll have to know who you are. But somehow I don't think you will. I'm quite sure you deliberately followed me into a deserted part of the garden and acted suspiciously to attract my attention. Then you refused to let the matter be dealt with quietly, your intention all along was to create a scandal in front of as many people as possible. If you're as respectable and honest as you say you are, why won't you tell me your name?"

"Because I am not wishink to tell you. Because you are mad, you will come to my house and make trouble for me." She struggled back into the fur coat. "You shall apologise. Now. At once."

"Not until you tell me your name and address."

"My name is Smith and I am livink at Buckingham Palace."

"Your real name and address."

"She is havink delusions, it is classic case of paranoia," the woman informed the company at large. "I am afraid she will attack me, therefore I go home now." She made off towards the car park, and Celia tried to follow. At least she could get the registration number of her car. But half a dozen people stepped forward to restrain her, advise her to be calm, leave well alone, forget the unfortunate mistake she had made.

Harriet confronted her like a symbolic figure of justice. "Celia, how could you humiliate me so? It was unforgivable."

"It was a trap, deliberately set for me to fall into. Why wouldn't she say who she was? Why didn't you make her?"

"Celia, I advise you to go home and lie down. And I beg you earnestly to see a psychiatrist as soon as possible, I am very worried about you."

Celia managed somehow not to hit her and began a dignified withdrawal from the scene. But after a few steps she broke into a run. With luck she might still be in time to see the number of the cyclamen-woman's car.

But when she reached the paddock where the cars were parked there was no movement to be seen except the roof of a grey car speeding down the lane on the far side of the hedge.

63

Right, Celia decided, from now on I don't sit and wait for things to happen, I turn detective. If necessary I forget about the garden maintenance contracts and let the cold frames fill with weeds, but I find out who is doing all this to me and I get him tried for murder.

Starting now, she decided, with a piece of routine checking. Months ago Deirdre had gone to her mother's for a weekend and left her phone number just in case. Surely it was written down somewhere? After a search of various likely surfaces she found it on her kitchen memo pad and rang it, expecting no reply.

"Hullo?" said a voice almost at once. But what was Deirdre's mother's surname?

"Good evening," she said. "I'm Celia Grant, I expect Deirdre's told you about me. I rang to find out how you are."

"I'm sorry, I must explain, I'm not Mrs Hurcomb, just a neighbour who comes in to water her plants while she's away. I happened to be here so I answered the phone."

"Then she's still in hospital?"

"No. I think there must be some mistake, she's away visiting her son in Canada. What made you think she was ill?"

Celia made an excuse and congratulated herself. Thanks to a bit of luck she had caught Timothy out. But an incoming call during the evening sent her misery-quotient shooting up again. She was faced with yet another search for a youth to cut grass, for Ron's father rang to say that Ron would not be turning up for work in the morning. No explanation or polite excuse, just an abrupt announcement. It could only mean one thing: the news of the fiasco at Harriet's had got round and fickle village opinion had turned against her. She was no longer the champion of the masses but a silly woman who had delusions about stolen cyclamens as well as dead bodies.

Her unhappiness-curve reached its climax at two in the morning when the telephone rang and a hoarse voice began whispering obscenities into her ear. Long ago she had worked out a drill for dealing with this nuisance if and when it happened, but being half-asleep she forgot it and slammed the phone down in its cradle. It started ringing again almost at once.

This time she was not caught unprepared. Without turning on the lights she groped her way downstairs to the office and switched in the Ansafone. The ringing stopped. Her recorded voice on the machine would be inviting the caller to record a message.

Despite her dressing gown she was shivering. It was easy to feel hard-boiled about obscene phone calls when deciding in the daytime how to deal with them. Sitting in a moonlit room while a machine recorded them was a different matter, especially with the nearest house a quarter of a mile away. Nor was this a call from some pathetic man who had picked a victim at random from the phone book. There was no way he could spot that "C S Grant, Archerscroft Nursery, Westfield" was the entry of a woman living alone. It had to be part of the hammering she was getting from the unknown person who had flown into a panic when she started to dig at The Towers.

It would be useful to have a recording of his voice, but had he recorded something? He might have decided it was too dangerous, in which case he would be furious with her for blocking his access to her with a machine. He had probably phoned from close at hand. His next step, perhaps, would be to attack the cottage.

The window of her office looked out at the back on to the yard and packing shed. The two vans threw sharp shadows in the moonlight which might contain anything, but there was no movement to be seen. The same applied on the side facing the lane. The front path and the wicket gate at the end of it were as bright as day, but anything could be lurking in the pitch black shadows of the yew trees to either side. Resisting the temptation to find out what was on the Ansafone, Celia decided to look to her defences.

When she moved in she had faced the fact that anyone determined enough could break into an isolated country cottage. There was a chain on the front door, but she had rejected suggestions of a burglar alarm as not worth it, for she had sold her jewellery and the silver to raise money for setting up the business. The important thing was to be able to sleep safely at night, so she had installed a heavy oak door fitted with steel bolts at the top of the stairs. She would be safe on the bedroom floor whatever was happening down below.

She shut herself into this upstairs fastness, but could not sleep, and moved to a chair by the window. In a way the moonlight made it worse. There would be no point in straining her eyes into black night, she could have drawn the curtains and hoped for the best. As it was she sat staring out of the window at the motionless trees and willing herself to stay calm.

When the noise started she did not realise at first where it came from. No one had come through the wicket gate and up the path between the two yew trees. But there was no doubt about it, someone hidden from sight under the porch was banging on the front door so hard that the whole cottage shook.

She picked up the bedside telephone to dial 999, then realised that the Ansafone was still switched in. To get through she would have to go downstairs and throw the switch. The noise was tremendous, should she risk it? The door was solid and would stand a lot of battering, but it would be childishly easy to break a window and climb in.

Why had her attacker not done just that? The answer, when it came to her, was a relief, but thank goodness she had not dialled 999. This was another trap. By the time the squad car came there would be nobody hammering on her door and no proof that anyone had been there. She would have chalked up another hallucination to her credit, and damaged her standing yet further with the police.

On thinking things over she decided that she was perfectly safe.

No damage would be done to life or property because her visitor would not want to leave evidence that she really was under attack and not a victim of her own heated imagination. She had only to sit tight and listen to a lot of noise until her visitor became exhausted and went away.

But before he went why not try to get a sight of him? That could not be managed from upstairs because of the overhanging porch. Under cover of a fresh bout of banging she unbolted the door at the top of the stairs and tiptoed down. The noise in the hall was even louder. She was tempted to lift the flap of the letterbox in the front door and peer through the slot, but decided against it for fear of what it might lead to.

The banging had become routine and desultory, as if he was wearily begging her to call the police so that he could cease his labours and go home to bed. Nothing could be seen of him through the living room window without opening it, which would lead to embarrassment on both sides, if not trouble. Under cover of another half-hearted burst of noise she slipped out of the back door and round the corner of the house. A *Camellia williamsii* in the shrub border at the front offered convenient cover. Hoping she was not trampling on too many lilies of the valley, she peered round it, getting an excellent view of the front porch.

He was neither tall nor short and dressed entirely in black. His head was a vague blackish blur in the deep shadow cast by the roof of the porch. He could be anybody, as he stood there exhausted by his efforts to be sinister and thumped on the door with a gloved hand from time to time.

She could see his head better now, silhouetted against the moonlit wall beyond. There was something curious about it, an odd vagueness of outline. What would happen if she spoke to him? "What on earth d'you think you're playing at?" would be an appropriate remark.

But she did not make it. With a muttered grunt of disgust he decided suddenly to give up. He turned, walked silently to the wicket gate and vaulted over it. Presently a car started somewhere down the lane.

Celia had said nothing. At the last moment she had lost her nerve. One did not say "What on earth d'you think you're playing at?" to a man in a stocking mask.

"So Mrs Foster's gone off," said Mrs Hallam as she prepared to wash Celia's kitchen floor. "Let you down proper, ain't she?"

Celia thought it best to stick to the official version: that what had let down all concerned was the collapse of Deirdre's mother's leg.

Mrs Hallam sniffed. "That's what Mrs Foster says. Gone off for a weekend with her fancy man if you ask me, only this time it's longer than the weekend." Her bucket was full and she turned off the tap. "Ain't you going to ask me who he is?"

This was no time, Celia thought, for ladylike scruples about not listening to gossip. "I expect you'll tell me anyway."

"Nigel Armitage. Been going on over a year."

This did not have to be taken seriously. Nigel was the village's fashionable all-purpose suspect, and Mrs Hallam had an imagination like a cesspit.

"S'true," she insisted. "Don't you believe me?"

"Of course not. Who spread it around that the new people at Elm Bank weren't married? You did, and everyone was terribly tactful about it, and now it turns out that she's his sister."

"That's right," said Mrs Hallam cheerfully. "Then they wouldn't be married, would they?"

Mrs Hallam was Ron's mother. Why had she turned up for work instead of sending her to Coventry like Ron? Curiosity no doubt. She would want to keep an observation post in Celia's camp so that she could spread stories of what went on there in all the other houses where she worked. But there was no point in being careful what one said in front of her: what was not said was easy to invent.

"Mind you I don't blame Mrs Foster," Mrs Hallam added. "Not with that husband of hers, the way he carries on. He's the pawing sort, not that he gets very far with them does he? He tried it on with that girl over at Barton Farm, and then it was that

68

divorced woman who went off to Australia, and after that, or was it before, it was Mrs Emerson."

Celia snapped to attention. "How d'you know?"

"Everyone knew. Mrs Emerson, she'd often drive down on the Friday morning to open up the cottage for the weekend, and Mr Foster was always hanging round Wheelwright's of a Friday before she went to pick up Mr Emerson off of the evening train."

"Mrs Hallam, are you sure about this?"

"'Course I'm sure, otherwise I wouldn't say. He'd come in the back way through Butler's Copse, so no one would see him."

"Did you actually see him coming through Butler's Copse?"

"Oh no, someone told me."

"Who?"

Mrs Hallam became vague. "Oh, I can't remember. 'S true, though."

That probably means she made it up, Celia thought. To grope further in this black hole of allegations would waste time she could not spare on a busy Monday morning, not with an ailing but urgently needed motor mower that must be got into intensive care at once.

Outside a grey sky promised rain later and made it hard to believe that the noisy carry-on in the night had ever happened. On the way to her van she stood for a moment at the corner of the house looking along the frontage to the porch. There was not a trace, not even a whisper on the Ansafone to prove that a man had stood there banging at her door. How tall was he? Shorter than he had seemed by moonlight, there had been a gap of fifteen inches at least between the top of his head and the overhanging porch roof. Five feet five at most, and good God yes, unisex, there was no proof that he was a man. Harriet Armitage in flat heels and a stocking mask? Too plump, and no stocking mask could disguise the square jaw and tremendous hair-do. The Fox-Norton woman or one of her horsy cronies? Possible. The whole witches' coven of them were cursing her guts for daring to suggest that their convenient murderer was inconveniently dead.

In Haxton, the local market town, she dumped the mower on a

69

repairer of agricultural machinery and put a small ad in the local paper, asking for someone to replace Deirdre. Not a pig's chance in a slaughterhouse of finding anyone suitable, but she had to try. The next problem was Bert Hodson's real estate dealings. The owner of the land between her cottage and the garden centre was a solicitor who, after the manner of his kind, was about to go into court and therefore could not be spoken to. Risking grievous bodily harm she blocked his escape route through his outer office and asked him if he had ever thought of selling.

"Why do you ask, Mrs Grant?"

"I might be interested."

"In making an offer? Or are you 'interested' because you have heard rumours?"

"Are there rumours to hear?"

"I suggest," he said, fiddling tetchily with his briefcase, "that you talk to Ringmere and Foster. I've put the matter in their hands."

So saying, he dodged about among the typists' desks and made his escape.

Goodness, so he is selling it to Hodson, Celia thought. Ringmere and Foster were the biggest land agents in the district, and Timothy Foster was one of the partners. Why had he not told her what was going on when she asked him yesterday? She would get him into a tizzy of embarrassment about that, then floor him by asking why he had lied about Deirdre's mother's broken leg.

But by the time she reached his office he had been warned and the secretaries had boiling oil ready to pour down on besiegers. He had somebody with him, he had to go out, he had a lunch date, would Mrs Grant like to see anyone else?

Who, she asked, was handling the sale of the land she was interested in?

Mr Foster was dealing with that personally. Had the land been sold, or was it still open to offer? Nobody knew, except Mr Foster. Was he in negotiation with a buyer, and if so who? Again, only Mr Foster could say. When would Mr Foster be available? No one could say.

70

Well, well. If Timothy would not tell her, perhaps Hodson would. Anyway, she meant to call in at the garden centre and take a look at Ethel Cooper's suspicious barn.

By the time she got there it had rained a little and the puddles in the cinder-strewn car park made it look scruffier than ever. She picked her way through a clutter of concrete Venuses and plastic lily-pools and into the vast sales shed full of fertilisers, poisons, seeds, pot plants and garden sundries, including plastic waterlilies to float in the plastic lily-pools. There were also closed-circuit television cameras and warnings about prosecuting thieves. Among the staff attending to customers or wheeling barrows about, the scowling young men with unkempt hair seemed to belong to the Hodson tribal culture. The girls, who were doing most of the work, were cheerful-looking and local. One of them on the checkout was from the village and recognised Celia. She made some sniggering remark to the girl on the next till, who turned and stared.

Celia walked through the shed to an outdoor sales area full of shrubs. As usual cheap rugosa rootstock was being sold for hedging at a vast price ("be the envy of your neighbours with a colour-packed hedge of sweet-scented rose blooms") and bare-root shrubs had been replanted in black plastic bags so that they could be passed off as container-grown. Celia pretended to interest herself in some miserable flowering cherries (genuinely container-grown, but the containers were infested with bitter cress) while inspecting the untidy clutter of greenhouses and sheds around her. There was nothing resembling a barn into which a large van could be driven, only a prefabricated metal shed with an up-and-over door like a garage door, except that it was high enough to take a good-sized truck. This had to be the building no one was allowed in, but it was a lot smaller than she had expected.

She strolled closer. It was windowless and the garage door had no handle. It must be controlled electrically or otherwise from within. But what went on inside? Nothing calling for a lot of room, certainly not "meetings" on the scale Ethel had suggested. By

71

Celia's reckoning the shed was less than thirty feet long, big enough to take a good sized van with a little to spare.

She would have liked to pace it out and make sure. But one of the Hodson tribesmen was gaping suspiciously at her behaviour; they seemed to be security guards rather than sales assistants. It would be wise to move on before he decided to beat her up.

Hodson's office was somewhere at the far end of the main sales shed. She headed that way, intending to batter the truth out of him if possible about the land sale, but a better option suddenly presented itself. Facing her from the other end of a long vista between sheds and greenhouses, was Timothy Foster.

He saw her at once but pretended not to and strolled out of sight behind the nearest greenhouse. A dignified hide-and-seek began, with Timothy breaking into a trot when he was out of sight behind buildings and slowing down again to a stroll when he saw her reappear at the end of some other vista. This went on for some time, till she rounded a corner expecting to see him close at hand, but found him gone. There was no shed or greenhouse in sight for him to be hiding behind, he had simply disappeared. Unless, of course, he had managed to break into the half-derelict building on her left.

It had been the Manor House till Hodson surrounded it with his garden centre. It was large and rambling, a glorified farmhouse added to from time to time, probably to cope with some Victorian family's mass production of children. It was now on the borderline between a house and a ruin and most of its windows were boarded up. What faced Celia seemed to be the kitchen wing, where some of the windows still held cobwebby glass. A door looked on closer inspection as if it might open, perhaps it was the entrance to some kind of store.

Put to the test the door did open on what was indeed a store. Cartons, some full and some empty, were tumbled about haphazard.

"Sorry lady, wholesale only in here," growled a voice behind her. A heavily bearded tribesman was glowering at her from behind a desk.

"I think Timothy Foster came in here," said Celia, peering around among the packing cases. "I wanted a word with him."

"There's only me here," said the tribesman.

"You must be mistaken, I'm sure Mr Foster came in here."

The tribesman came round his desk and stood very close to her, exuding an unwashed smell. "This is wholesale only in here," he said loudly, as if repeating a lesson. "You better go, there's no one here but me."

But this was no longer true, for the door behind her had opened and two men had come in together, talking in low tones. One of them was her accountant, Peter Hewlett, the other she did not know. When they saw her they stopped talking at once. There seemed to be some kind of crisis.

"Good morning Mr Hewlett," the tribesman blurted out, "I . . . had a word with Mr Hodson and he says he can give you wholesale terms. I have the invoice here . . ."

But his desk was blank. There was nowhere much that an invoice could be produced from. Everyone stared at Celia, her being there was an outrage. Nothing more would happen till she left.

She gave Hewlett a curt nod and went out. So Ethel had got it wrong, the "meetings" were held in the derelict manor, not in the taboo shed which was visited by the truck. The desk was a reception desk and security barrier, there must be a door somewhere behind the piles of cartons which admitted the elect to an inner room. What sort of meetings though? Sales conferences of commercial travellers in heroin? Surely not, Peter Hewlett was a churchwarden and borough councillor. Accomplices of the power-crazed Bert Hodson, who was plotting to hold the world to ransom with laser beams? Not credible. But he was up to something murky, calling for a furtive back entrance as an essential business asset. No wonder he wanted her cottage and the land. But if she asked him why, he would only dish up a lot of nonsense, and Timothy would melt into a puddle of grease rather than tell her. There was no point in hanging around, she had better go.

73

Apart from that, two very hostile tribesmen were glowering at her from the corners of widely separated sheds. She had offended against tribal custom by forcing her way into a taboo area. As she walked towards the car park they took up station warily behind her like sheepdogs dealing with a stray ewe which must be shooed back into the flock. When she reached the car park they stood on the edge of it, still glowering. If she did not drive away at once they would begin to bark.

But one of them seemed to have caught sight of something alarming down on the main road. He gave the other a startled nudge, and they hurried across the car park towards Celia, who was making a great thing of finding her car keys and peering over the top of her handbag to see what the panic was about.

Down on the main road a whitish truck with nothing written on its blank sides was circling the roundabout. It turned in at the entrance and headed up past the car park into the garden centre. It had to be the truck from the taboo shed because the tribesmen were now making frantic efforts to divert her attention from it.

"It's silly to poke your nose into other people's business, dear."

"Thass right dear, it's not safe."

"Mister Hodson says you're not to come pokin' round here any more or he'll punish you, see?"

"So watch out then if you don't want a broken face."

But Celia's misery-quotient was not shooting up as they would have wished. She was too busy repeating the truck's registration number over and over again in her head. When she had escaped to the relative safety of a busy main road full of fast traffic she pulled into a lay-by and wrote it down. It had vanished so fast into the mysterious shed that there had been no chance to take in much else about it, except that it looked like a non-standard job built or adapted for a special purpose. It had some kind of complicated ventilator or air-conditioner installed on its roof. Why? What on earth was Hodson up to?

Back at Archerscroft Celia munched bread and cheese and wondered what to detect next. Inspiration came to her and she rang a friend who had employed a detective agency to trace children spirited away by an ex-husband. Having got the address and telephone number she commissioned the agency to shadow the white van on its next journey, trace it to its destination and if possible discover what its contents were. It would be expensive, but worth the money. To trundle along behind the white van in her own very recognisable little pick-up would be futile and possibly dangerous.

Further action must await the detective agency's report, so she buckled down to two days of intensive horticulture. A quick look round the frame yard showed that three more of the double primroses were fully out with a single bloom or two on each, so they would probably set seed. One was a self-coloured crimson, another an orange-bordered scarlet, a third a rather sickly mauve flecked with brick red. The sight of them was the only cheering thing that had happened for days.

A huge effort brought the maintenance contracts under control. At the end of a long morning's slog of weeding and mowing and carting away rubbish she dropped in on Ethel Cooper, utterly worn out.

"I'm exhausted, Ethel. It's slavery without Deirdre and Ron's given me notice. Can you think of anyone who'd help me out for a bit?"

Ethel hesitated, went pink, and did not look at her. "No dear," she said gently.

How awful, I've embarrassed her, Celia thought. No one would want to work for her after the fiasco at the Old Rectory.

"I still believe in you, Celia," said Ethel. "That woman stole the plant to set a trap for you, I'm sure."

"But who's behind it? Who's doing all this?"

"Nigel Fitzgerald. I told you. He's the one that does those silly jokes."

"But he does have an alibi for the murder. My guess is Bert Hodson. You were right, I went up there, something is going on."

"You mean what Mrs Clay's youngest told me, about the funny meetings?"

"Yes, but I think that happens in the old manor house. The shed where the truck goes in and out isn't big enough."

"Does it, dear? Then I got it wrong."

"What does go on in the shed, though?"

"Nothing, according to the little Clay girl, I had a word with her. She's only repeating what the others say, it may be a lot of gossip and no one gets a good look because those rough men of Hodson's try to keep everyone away. What they say is, if you peek in when the doors open to let the truck out, nothing's there that wasn't there before."

"Then what's in there, apart from the truck when it comes?"

"Nothing, she says, just bare walls."

"Hm. What a weird carry-on."

"Yes. A glass of sherry dear, to cheer us up?"

"Thanks, but I must get back, there's so much to do."

While she was watering and catching up on odd jobs in the frame yard a helmeted figure rode in from the lane on what even she could see was a very expensive motorcycle. He dismounted, unzipped his leather jacket and brought out a copy of the local paper.

"Hullo there. Nice day," he said. "Would you be the lady that put the ad in the paper about a job?"

He took off his helmet and shook out what looked like a very expensive haircut. He was well-built, embarrassingly handsome, and not a day over twenty. "If you're not suited yet, I'd like to apply."

Goodness, thought Celia. At best she had hoped for an old age pensioner full of earthy lore about dahlias, and here was the Apollo Belvedere clad in de luxe leather goods. What with the expensive motorcycle and all it was highly suspicious.

Then it hit her. This was why Deirdre Foster had been whisked away. That had always puzzled her, but it was as clear as daylight now. It was to make a vacancy for this star-wars saboteur to slide into so that he could get inside her defences and send her distress-factor up even higher. She was desperate for a helping hand to replace Deirdre but no, not as desperate as that.

"What's your name?" she snapped.

This seemed to call for a moment's thought. "Bill Williams." Bill Williams. What a name to invent.

"What's yours?" he asked.

"Celia Grant. What d'you know about gardening?"

He grinned, looking disgustingly healthy and confident. "Try me out, Celia, why don't you?"

Right, she thought. Something tricky to flummox him and give her an excuse for throwing him out on his ear. Ah yes, a little weeding. In the seed beds.

On the way there they passed the open door of the greenhouse. Just inside on the staging was a batch of fancy zonal perlargoniums with a distinctive yellow leaf.

"They're nice, unusual," said Bill and flicked one of the pots with a fingernail. "Needs water." He flicked two more. "Those are okay."

You little show off, Celia thought. Where did you learn that bit of old world gardeners' lore? She led him in silence to a neglected patch at the end of the row of seed-beds. All sorts of interesting things had seeded themselves in it, but also chickweed and bitter cress and all manner of buggins, and as she had not had any time it had degenerated into a little hell. She marked out a patch a yard square with a stick and told him to weed it without taking out anything that wasn't a weed. He nodded, pulled off the leather jacket and rolled up his sleeves.

When he squatted down and began work Celia had a bird's-eye view of his hair-do. The rich brown curls had to be dyed—the colour was too even, darker than his lashes and eyebrows and much darker than the almost white hairs glinting on his forearms. He was a crypto-blonde, and who would go darker out of vanity? And not very recently, the dye had begun to grow out at the roots. He was in disguise, but why?

"Now Celia," he said. "Let's see what we have here."

Nothing of importance had gone from his patch, but he had cleared off the large weeds and was picking out the small ones. As his weeding-tool moved about competently among the seedlings he began a running commentary. "Those are some sort of little pansies or violas, we'll leave them, and that stinking hellebore. There's lots of hellebores in here, the orientals and the big green one with the shiny leaf from Corsica. Those look to me like foxtail lilies, is that right?"

"Yes. You're not taking out that little briar seedling?"

"No Celia, that's not a wild rose, it's the one with the grey leaf, it's *Rosa rubrifolia*. The birds take the hips and drop the seeds all over, but they're nice. And this in the corner here, it looks like an ordinary spear thistle, but it's not, not with the the two long green leaves sticking out."

"What is it then?"

"Ah, it's that great grey thistle with the purple flowers that grows eight feet tall the second year and dies. Ono-something, they call it."

What anguish, Celia thought, having to turn away a man who recognised an *Onopordon arabicum* seedling two inches across. But it was such an obvious trap, he looked like a messenger of death from some pretentious film. If she hired him she would be rigid with terror day and night.

"You realise I can only afford the basic agricultural wage?" she growled.

"That's okay, Celia. I'd not expect more."

Naturally. Someone else was paying him far more than that for roughing her up rotten.

"Are you sure?" she said. "You look expensive to me."

A flicker of bad temper crossed his face. If she queried his good faith, not that he had any, he would turn ugly.

"You've got your insurance card and P64?"

"No, I'd have to get all that."

Of course. His papers would show where he'd worked last, for all she knew he was straight from prison. She would stall and ask him to produce them.

Or would she? Why struggle on without help? That would end her up in traction for a slipped disc if the mental hospital did not get her first. Why not hire him and watch him for dirty tricks? It

78

would be terrifying, but where was the extra risk? If the idea was to bash her on the head and Paraquat the cold frames, sending him away would not stop it. There were plenty of other ways the dirty tricks department could get at her.

"Come in and have some coffee," she said, still undecided, "and we'll talk."

On the way in he paused by the double primroses. "They're nice, I've not seen them before. Where did you get them?"

"I bred them."

"It's nice, breeding things."

Had he been briefed to steal them? Had be been here before, banging on her front door in a stocking mask? In a way it would be less terrifying to have the danger under her eye, instead of wondering every moment where it was coming from and when it would strike. It would be a battle of wits. She would pretend to suspect nothing and worm information out of him. If the worming went well it might yield a hard fact or two, some clue. She was sick of groping about in a fog of village gossip.

"What did you say your name was?" she asked as they settled down in the kitchen over their coffee.

He remembered almost at once that it was Bill Williams.

"Where did you train?"

Not, it seemed, at a horticultural college. He claimed to have been garden boy, then under-gardener at a house near Rugeley called The Grange, owned by a couple called Wilson. He had learnt all he knew from their holy terror of a head gardener, who was called McTavish. The Wilsons were both dead and the house was now an old people's home.

This was not believable, nor even intended to be. The McTavish bit was pure caricature, it was his way of saying "don't be naive and ask for references". His face had set in a fierce pretty-boy sulk, daring her to ask awkward questions.

They had finished their coffee. He was waiting, but she still dithered. Yes or no? "No" was less risky, but "yes" offered a faint hope of finding out something solid at last.

"Can you start tomorrow?" she said.

SEVEN

THAT AFTERNOON CELIA'S image took another bashing. Her van broke down very publicly in the village street, with its engine belching steam at an interested crowd of spectators. Jim from the petrol pumps swaggered over the road to display his expertise and told all concerned that the cylinder block had cracked on account of no water in the radiator and no oil in the sump. Celia had checked both the day before—she was terrified of garage bills and always took care. Someone (could it have been "Bill Williams"?) must have visited her in the night and drained off the oil and water as the van stood in the yard. But what was the point of telling the village that? It would sound like yet another feeble fairy story from poor half-mad Mrs Grant. Much wiser to keep quiet and become a feckless goose who could not look after machinery properly.

Feeling far from better on reaching this conclusion she was wondering what to do about the broken-down van when Lucinda Fox-Norton came out of the village shop with a great grin all over her lantern jaw.

"Ah Celia, good news," she said, fixing her with evil glee. "Haven't you heard? Ethel Cooper's had a letter from Kenny."

The crowd was looking at her with the sullen excitement of onlookers at a fatal street accident. Someone sniggered. In a vivid moment Celia saw herself as the village must see her, a self-appointed detective who had been exposed as a failure in addition to being completely mad.

Feeling ridiculous from head to foot, she stammered, "I must talk to Ethel," and turned tail.

Distressingly, Ethel seemed embarrassed rather than angry.

"Anyone can make a mistake Celia," she said, trying to be kind. "Only it did upset me, you saying he was dead."

"I know. I'm sorry."

Kenny's letter was written in capitals teetering drunkenly along a ruled pencil line in spelling that Chaucer would have thought unorthodox. DEAR MUM I AM FIN AND HOP YOU ARE I NEVER DONE THEM PEEPL AT WEELRITS BUT I NO I GET THE BLAM THATS WY I RUN AWAY YOR LOVIN SON KENNY.

It was posted in central London.

"I don't know what to say to you, Celia," said Ethel, even more embarrassed.

Celia knew what she must not say to Ethel: Kenny was almost illiterate and surely knew her phone number so why had he not sidestepped the agony of writing a letter and phoned her? Was this his writing? A forged letter was such an obvious move if he could not be produced alive, and who could prove it was a forgery? Even if Ethel could produce a specimen of his writing for comparison, what handwriting expert would say yes or no about two sets of barely literate block capitals?

But there was one thing she had to say. "Ethel, you won't let too many people handle Kenny's letter, will you?"

"Why not?"

"When you show it to the police they'll want to test it for fingerprints."

"I don't understand."

"If Kenny's prints are on it they'll know it really is from him."

This seemed to take forever to sink in. When Ethel grasped what she was hinting at her face went grim. "Get away with you, Celia," she said harshly. "You've upset me enough already with your interfering. I don't want to talk to you about Kenny, not ever again."

Celia spent a miserable night. Having the village against her was bad enough, but Ethel Cooper was a friend. That really hurt, and finding that the little pick-up that Ron and Deirdre had been using was also empty of water and oil did not help her morale. When Bill Williams arrived in the morning to start work she felt even worse.

Why on earth had she hired a built-in threat to her physical safety and peace of mind? And when he walked into the kitchen in his working clothes another reason for not hiring him presented itself. He looked like a body-building advertisement in his singlet and jeans. Mrs Hallam was barely continent with excitement as she added him to her gossip repertoire, probably as the object of a carnal passion disgusting at Celia's age. She was past caring what Mrs Hallam spread around the village about her, but saw a danger she had not thought of before. Had this scrumptious young man been sent to compromise her sexually, destroy her credibility once for all by accusing her of rape and provoking a huge scandal? She would be wise to keep her distance and avoid being alone with him on enclosed premises.

But he turned out to be a quick worker, and showed no signs of becoming over-familiar. By the end of the day they had weeded most of the seed-beds and caught up on one of the outstanding garden contracts. They chatted while they worked, Celia saw to that. His flat, almost classless, speech told one nothing—it could be protective colouring for almost any social background including the criminal underworld. But she was gradually forced to the conclusion that though "The Grange" was fictitious, McTavish, probably under another name, was real. He had certainly trained under a working gardener—there were gaps in his knowledge which a course at a horticultural college would have filled—and only a novelist with a very fertile imagination could have invented McTavish, who sounded a richly eccentric character. The Wilsons, his employers, emerged as shadowy figures by comparison. What happened to him after he left "The Grange" seemed to be a forbidden topic, and he switched on the pretty-boy sulk when she pressed him. It was a relief when he went off home to his lodgings in Haxton at four o'clock on his sumptuous motorcycle. She felt safer without him.

Next morning she set him to work and drove into Haxton herself. The damaged mower was ready to collect and a roll of film had to be dropped in on a friendly photographer to be developed.

"More of your interesting flower studies, Mrs Grant?"

82

"No, they're mostly of a beautiful young man with no shirt on, but don't get ideas. I'm employing him and I think he's a criminal so I took them without him knowing, in case. But he was working with his shirt off, I couldn't ask him to put it on again, could I?"

"Of course not." The photographer smiled indulgently.

I'm an idiot, thought Celia, never apologise, never explain. I hope to God the waistband of his jeans is in the pictures.

Her camera was a good one with a telephoto lens. While Bill was barrowing compost to a new seed-bed she was making, she had taken four or five shots of him from the shelter of the potting shed. The last time was a narrow squeak, he heard the click of the camera and looked round suspiciously. For a moment she even thought he was coming to investigate.

No fresh savagery had been unleashed on her since the sabotaging of the van and the pick-up, and this in itself was unnerving. She still had no clue as to why he had been planted on her, or what foul trick he had been briefed to play. Nor had he betrayed by the flicker of an eyelid that he knew all about the events that had rocked the village over the past few days. One of her Friday chores was to make the garden at The Towers look less like a jungle. She had been dreading the idea of going back to the scene of her gruesome discovery, especially with a spy from the enemy camp sitting beside her in the pick-up. He made no comment as they drove up the gloomy drive between the massed rhododendrons. She longed to know what was going on in his brain.

With two mowers in rude health they could make short work of the grass-cutting. She set him to work on the upper lawn and went down to the lower one herself, ostensibly to mow but in fact to tidy up the fateful herbaceous border without him looking on. If they started to discuss the whys and wherefores of the gaping upheaval in it, the whole tense situation would probably explode.

Seeing it again in the daylight did not make her feel any better or any less sure that she had seen Kenny's foot. The whole area with its encircling trees seemed haunted still by Kenny's presence and she even caught (or was she imagining it?) a faint lingering whiff of

83

the smell of death. The decaying corpse of the crow was nowhere to be found, perhaps the police had taken it away.

By midday they had finished the grass-cutting and rested in the shade. Bill looked up into the canopy of leaves. "That's a tulip tree up there. There was one at The Grange, on the front lawn. Lovely in the autumn it was, all yellow."

"Were there a lot of good trees?"

"Magnolias, there was lovely magnolias, like here." He looked around. "There was a special one I liked, I've not seen it here, with white flowers facing down instead of up and red stamens and things in the middle."

This was riveting. Was The Grange real after all? Afraid of alarming him, she went on putting questions as casually as she could. Eucryphias, yes, they were lovely in August, weren't they, when nothing much else was out. Wisteria . . . a walled rose garden. By the end of the day she had built up a fairly complete picture of a medium-sized garden with a goodish tree and shrub collection and a lot of interesting features. Some of them rang a bell in her mind, especially the magnolia with the downward-pointing flowers. It had a circular seat round its trunk, so that one could sit and look up into the flowers. She had seen that somewhere, a *Magnolia sinensis* with a seat round it, in one of the umpteen gardens she had visited with Roger, but which? The Grange, near Rugeley? It meant nothing to her. She tried to make Bill describe the house, but he switched on the pretty-boy sulk and clammed up on her in a panic, he realised he'd said too much.

Punctually at four she sent him off for the weekend, she could get through Saturday without shelling out for him on overtime. It would be nice to stop wondering for a bit what hellish trick he was going to pull and when. After he had gone she took down the Geological Atlas of Great Britain and confirmed her hunch that "The Grange" did not exist. According to Bill the garden there was on greensand, and there was not a speck of greensand within twenty miles of Rugeley. So he had trained at a house not called "The Grange" under a gardener not called McTavish and something frightful had happened, followed by a prison sentence.

84

It must be that, otherwise why the uptight silence about what happened after he left there? She was on to something concrete at last, all she had to do was remember where she had seen a *Magnolia sinensis* with a circular seat round its trunk.

She could see it now, in a kind of dell, a biggish one with a spread of at least twenty feet. It must have been planted soon after they were introduced from China in 1908. But where on earth was it? Its image haunted her throughout Saturday, and after the last customer had left she drove up to The Towers to consult the only person within reach who might know, namely the widow of that authoritative plantsman Sir Henry Armitage.

She parked in the yard. Nigel looked out from an upstairs window in the coach house.

"Hullo there, Celia. The village is ringing with your latest exploits."

"Oh, which in particular?"

"Lesbianism as usual, and heterosexual baby-snatching."

"I see. Are these alternative theories, or am I omnivorous?"

"I'm not sure, but you should have hired someone uglier to push that lawnmower about."

"The point is, he can weed a seedbed without vandalising it. When Deirdre fled from my loathsome embraces I had to replace her with someone. Where is Deirdre?"

He looked surprised. "What makes you think I'd know?"

"The buzz in the village is that she finds your embraces less loathsome than mine."

"Then the buzz is wrong. Does Kenny Cooper's resurrection embarrass you?"

"My dear Nigel, I'm past being embarrassed by anything short of the Last Judgement." She turned to go into the house.

"Were you hoping to penetrate the defences?" Nigel asked.

"Yes, I want to pick your grandmother's brains, if I can get past Alison."

"You'll have a job. To paraphrase the bard, 'Celia, thou hast my mother much offended,' with that tasteless exhumation of nothing from the herbaceous border."

85

Celia too doubted if she would be let in, and even Boxie looked dubious as she unlocked the door. "I'll ask," she said.

Celia waited. The cinerarias had gone from the bamboo flower-stand. They had been replaced by a massed bank of heliotrope, backed by stephanotis trained up a wire frame. The air was heavy with their combined scent. Alison came out into the hall as usual, but she looked like a terminal case of indigestion. She had gone sharply downhill since Celia saw her last.

"How dare you come here. Mother doesn't want to see you," she said in a kind of faint moaning hiss.

"Oh yes I do." Nellie herself had come hobbling on two sticks out of a door further down the hall. "Come in, Celia dear."

She and Alison glared at each other. The tension was electric. It was clear that Celia had interrupted a quarrel, they were making no attempt to hide it.

"Alison, you really are a fool," said Nellie. "Go and help Boxie get the tea."

"Very well, mother," said Alison, but not in her usual weary-submissive tone. With a defiant glare at Nellie she followed Boxie towards the kitchen premises.

Nellie was blinking away angry tears, it looked as if she had just lost a battle of wills. She led the way into her sitting room, which was very hot, though the fire in the grate had been let out.

After giving Celia a woebegone look, she burst into a sudden cackle. "So there wasn't a corpse in that border. Pity, we could have opened the garden in aid of the district nurses and charged fifty pence to gape into the hole where it was found, or do you think . . ."

"Nellie, you must be kinder to Alison, she looks like death."

The old lady became tetchy again. "Don't interrupt me and don't bully me, I'm too old to be bullied. There's nothing wrong with Alison except that yesterday when that noble savage of yours was gardening here with his shirt off she was at her bedroom window all day with my opera glasses making herself ill with lust."

"She doesn't look at all well. Has she seen her doctor?"

"Of course, what good does that do? Tell the young man to keep his shirt on and wear a false nose, like the pretty girl in the story who had to because the men couldn't control themselves. Where did you find him?"

"There's a mystery about that. I've come to pick your brains about it," said Celia, and explained about "The Grange".

"A *Magnolia sinensis* with a seat round it," Nellie mused. "Yes, that does ring a bell."

"And a carriage sweep in front of the house with a big tulip tree in the middle of a lawn."

"That doesn't, it could be anywhere. Tell me more."

"The rose garden has four eucryphias in the middle round some kind of statue."

"I've seen that somewhere too, and thought what a good idea. Liven things up in August while the roses are resting. How big is this garden?"

"About four acres, he says. There's a formal courtyard garden with a lily pool in the middle and a wisteria trained over a wire gazebo and big mixed borders round the walls . . ."

"Stone or brick?"

"Stone."

"What's the house like?"

"No idea, he won't say. There's what sounds like an interesting wild garden with a stream down the middle and a good shrub collection . . ."

"Rhododendrons?"

"Only in moderation, it's not one of those dingy green hells that suddenly look like the remnant counter at Liberty's in May."

"Ah. What about lobelia and scarlet geraniums and so on?"

"Absolutely not, all the municipal flowers were taboo. Mr Wilson had refined tastes, there were frightful rows about geraniums with McTavish."

"What sort of roses?"

"Old-fashioned, and the pale kinds that tumble picturesquely over immemorial stone walls. No violent colours, and no vulgar hybrid teas like Peace or Superstar."

"Was this Wilson person married?"

"Yes, but I'm sure he's fictitious. Why?"

"It sounds like a queer's garden to me—wait! I've had an idea."

Alison came in with a loaded tea-tray.

"I know where this house is, it's in Berkshire somewhere," said Nellie. "Why am I so damned old, I forget everything, what was the man's name?" She closed her eyes. "Talk about something else and it will come back to me."

Celia moved a pile of books off the table for Alison to put down the tray. Under it was one of Nellie's enchanting flower paintings, a pageful of watercolour studies of an unusual nasturtium.

"This isn't the ordinary *Tropaeolum majus*," she said. "What is it?"

But Nellie's mind was elsewhere. "Got it!" she cried. "The house is called Fontbury and it belongs to a little cad called Richard Chatham."

At this, Alison dropped her tray of tea things and began to scream and scream.

EIGHT

THE SCREAMS TURNED into whooping-cough type laughter, in more and more strident spasms.

"The high-strikes," Nellie grumbled. "Slap her face."

Celia stepped over the ruins of afternoon tea for three and did so.

"That's no good, harder," said Nellie.

Celia redoubled her efforts. "Stop it, Alison. Stop it at once, d'you hear?"

Far from complying Alison flung herself on the floor and drummed with her heels among the tea things.

"Cold water," Nellie prescribed. "In her face, a whole bucketful."

Celia sprang to obey. Nigel was just outside the door. She ran slap into him but dodged past into the passage.

He tried to grab her. "Where are you going?"

"To get water, your mother's having hysterics."

"Celia, come back," he shouted.

She ran on down the passage towards the kitchen. At the end of it Boxie blocked her path, looking alarmed. "What are you doing down here?"

"Draw me a bucket of cold water, quick."

Boxie did not move. Something must be happening in the kitchen that Celia was not meant to see.

Nigel came bounding towards them down the passage. "I'm sorry, Celia, mother's in a frightful state of nerves, she's taken against you. It's not your fault, but you'd better go."

"Very well, but attend to your mother first. Boxie, do get that water."

"I'll attend to that," said Nigel. "Boxie will let you out."

They looked at her with set faces, waiting for her to move. She turned to follow Boxie and Nigel went to the kitchen sink to fill a bucket. A quick glance into the kitchen suggested that nothing sensational was happening there, only something cooking on the stove which smelt overpoweringly of onions. Alison's screeching laughter still rang out, and over it a man's voice shouted, "What the hell's going on up there?" It seemed to come from the back staircase. Celia paused as she passed it, but Boxie hurried her on with a savage pull at her arm. "Mind your own business for once, can't you?"

She hobbled to the front door and went through the routine of letting Celia out. In the doorway Celia paused, searching for something conciliatory to say. But Boxie gave her a push. "Be off with you and let me get back to Miss Alison."

Celia drove away. The last few minutes had been rich in interest and she began sorting out her impressions. For instance, Nigel had been listening at the door during Celia's conversation with Nellie about Bill Williams and the mysterious garden. He must have been, because when she ran slap into him he was standing outside the door like the Commendatore's statue in Don Juan, not hurrying in.

Next, nobody had asked what on earth was wrong with Alison, looking after her was a low priority. Priority number one was getting Celia out of the house before Alison recovered her speech and let slip something disastrous.

But it was more complex than that. Nigel had said, "Come back," and Boxie had said, "What are you doing down here?" When Celia glanced up the back staircase Boxie had hurried her past it and said, "Mind your own business." There was something down in the kitchen quarters that they did not want her to see, and she knew what it was: the heavy steel rail at one side of the staircase at skirting level, and the chair clamped to it at the bottom ready to take a disabled person up.

Celia had not known the chair-lift existed. The theory was that Nellie was confined to the ground floor. She remembered now, once or twice when she had been kept waiting a faint whirring in the back premises had puzzled her. That was Nellie riding downstairs, so that she could be produced sitting in the morning room as if she had never moved from it. So she had the run of the first floor, but why was it such a secret?

Finally there was the voice in the back premises which had shouted, "What's going on?" She was almost sure it was Roy Armitage's.

She glanced at her watch. If she drove hell for leather she could collect the roll of film from the photographer's in Haxton before he shut. Tomorrow was Sunday, she would make an expedition.

"Wilkins, not Williams," Richard Chatham corrected as he studied the photographs. "I think his name was Bill, but he was always Wilkins to me."

Celia sipped her coffee. She remembered Chatham perfectly now, and Fontbury, a small Queen Anne manor house with marvellous ceilings and fireplaces. Chatham had just inherited it, and invited Roger over to advise him on the garden with its collection of exotic trees. Then, Chatham had been a too-rich, too-handsome young man with nothing to do but have perfect taste. He had become a sleek middle-aged bachelor with a houseful of beautiful things, flawlessly kept by a youngish manservant who was not sinister unless one thought about it. The tour round the garden before lunch had been a real treat, he was knowledgeable and imaginative and genuinely fond of flowers but without gush. The lunch had been far too delicious to spoil by talking business over it, so she had left the nitty-gritty till now.

"But what's happened to his hair, it's disastrous," said Chatham, looking at the pictures again.

"He's dyed it. That was one of the things that made me suspicious."

"The Grange at Rugeley," he mused. "And McTavish, dear me."

There was a longish silence.

"Let me get this clear, Mrs Grant. He's been planted on you,

91

he's lied to you, there's a murder mystery in the background and you're terrified of him."

"That's roughly it, yes."

"It's possible he's turned to crime. I wouldn't blame him after what happened here. I shall have to tell you a story I'm not proud of, so please keep it to yourself if you can."

After another short pause he plunged in. "Wilkins was so beautiful, you see, the Michaelangelo David seemed coarse by comparison. I couldn't really afford an under-gardener, but equally, I couldn't bear the thought of turning him away. He was nicer than any garden ornament, I enormously enjoyed just watching him working away so seriously and looking so happy over it. He loved gardens and gardening and he was so eager to learn.

"Then one day like an idiot, I can't think what came over me, I went mad and made a pass at him. Quite a mild one, but he was utterly bewildered and shocked and disgusted, you can imagine the fuss. And he rushed off to tell his father who came rushing back here to see me.

"By that time I was terrified, because Wilkins was under age and I'd attempted to commit a criminal offence. If Papa had realised that and gone to the police I'd have been in deep trouble. But fortunately he was rather dim and . . . oh dear, this is the part I'm really ashamed of.

"I was desperate, you see. I had to make up some story because if it got round the village that I'd interfered with a minor I'd never have a moment's peace again. So I managed to convince Papa, who as I say was rather dim, that I'd caught Wilkins coming out of my bedroom with my watch and cufflinks and a lot of money from my wallet in his pocket; whereupon he'd made up this filthy story to discourage me from calling in the police.

"So Papa went off satisfied. But next morning Wilkins barged in here in a towering rage, I'd no idea he had such a temper. He had a sad little cardboard suitcase with him, and he said he was leaving home for good because he was furious with his father for taking my word against his. Of course he was furious with me too. He ordered me to sit down and write him a testimonial so that he could get another job, but I couldn't do that without admitting that I'd lied about him stealing and his story about me was true. I refused, whereupon he very sensibly made a thorough job of knocking me down, and promised to repeat the process as necessary till I changed my mind.

"This was a bit embarrassing because a houseful of weekend guests had just arrived. But by the greatest of good luck one of them was Sandra Morrison. She was the sort of woman one can tell about that sort of predicament, and better still, she runs an agency for photographic models in West Molton Street. I told her how beautiful Wilkins was, so she went to have a look and tried to make him strip off, which he flatly refused to do and I don't blame him in the circumstances. But it seems there was a shortage at the time of virile-looking persons who photographed really well, so she thrust a fiver into his hand and told him to report to West Molton Street on Monday morning and earn untold wealth.

"That's the last I've seen of him, except in bathing trunks on escalators in the tube, or modelling beachwear in the Sunday supplements or on great hoardings in something to do with beer, and so on and so on. I think you'd have recognised him if he'd left his hair alone, it's the palest possible gold."

"I suppose this is why he can afford the expensive motorbike," said Celia.

"Of course. For a few years they make an enormous amount of money, but I can't forgive myself for letting anything so awful happen to him."

"Oh? It sounds as if you did him a good turn."

"My dear Mrs Grant, how little you know. It's the sleaziest milieu imaginable. Handsome men who let themselves be photographed for money are the lowest of the low in the advertising world. Even the lighting and props men despise them and the art directors treat them like cattle. Most of them are muscle-freaks or narcissists or odd in some other way and they're assumed to be up for grabs sexually by anyone in the hiring and firing department. I hate to think of poor little Wilkins caught up in that world. If he's drifted from there into crime it's my fault. Please let me know what happens, I'm very worried about this."

"Of course, and thank you for being so frank. May I ask you now about something else? Does the name of Alison Fitzgerald mean anything to you?"

He searched his memory. "Not that I remember."

"And . . . do forgive me, but she has a son, quite a good-looking boy in his twenties, called Nigel."

"Thank you for putting it so delicately, but no."

"Alison is the daughter of Sir Henry and Lady Armitage, perhaps . . ."

"Oh. Yes, the plant collector, I've met them. They came here once years ago, they were friends of my father and wanted to see what I'd done to the garden. They approved of the garden but not of me, not virile enough, and I haven't seen them since."

"This is rather important, you're sure you've had no other dealings with that family?"

He thought again. "Quite sure. Why?"

"Your name seemed to ring a bell with Alison Fitzgerald."

"Dear me, what sort of a bell?"

"She screamed and dropped a tray when your name was mentioned."

"I see, more like cymbals than a bell. What an eventful life you lead." He rose and went over to his desk. "You'll want Sandra Morrison's phone number. I'll find it for you, but do please let me know what you find out about Wilkins."

Celia glanced furiously at her watch and went back to the cottage to phone again. Even on a Monday morning people in London ought surely to be in their offices by twenty-past-ten.

She had been working away with grim desperation in the packing shed since eight, getting the week's orders ready for dispatch. Her woe-coefficient was bumping against the roof. Bill had not turned up for work. The double primroses had vanished from their cold frame and he had smashed its glass as a parting gesture. What an anti-climax, it was infuriating. She had gone in terror of him for days and all he had done was smash a few panes of glass and steal some plants. Mercifully she had not told him that the *corsicus* hybrids in the hellebore seedbed were much more valuable than the primroses.

Mrs Hallam was agog with innuendo on learning of these developments. No doubt Bill's embarrassed refusal to be seduced by his employer would be the next instalment of her *Dallas*-style village soap opera.

Celia dialled Sandra Morrison's number again. This time there was a reply. She gave her name and was put through.

"Good morning, Mrs Grant. Richard Chatham phoned me. It's about Bill Wilkins, I gather."

"That's right. Can you give me any background on him?"

"I'll try, but I don't know much about him really, he kept himself to himself. However, here goes: He's got a temper and he's fanatically chaste sexually. Men who tried anything on with him got knocked down and he stood no nonsense from women art directors who fancied him, I had to warn them about that. But it didn't hold him back because he was a very good model, very organised and conscientious and very relaxed in front of the cameras."

"What about his private life?"

"I'm sorry, I've no idea. I try to look after the girls a bit, especially the very young ones. But frankly, male models are mostly so odd that I try not to know what they get up to."

"Could there be a criminal connection somewhere in the background?"

"As I rather suggested, anything's possible. In his case it wouldn't surprise me. He was a loner, didn't say much, didn't mix. People were a bit afraid of him, because of his temper."

"What sort of things touched it off?"

"Insults to his dignity, and attempts to involve him in casual sex. But he was all right most of the time. I was sorry to lose him."

"You mean, he's no longer on your books?"

"Sorry, I thought you knew. He came in here a month ago with his hair dyed a hideous brown and said he'd hated every minute of being a model and only did it for the money. And now he'd saved enough so he was getting out."

"Did he say what he was going to do?"

"Yes. I asked in a fit of social conscience, because he must have saved twenty thousand at least and it's a lot of money for a kid like that to go on the loose with. It turned out that he wanted to go back into gardening, but of course he had no reference as a gardener because Richard Chatham had refused to give him one. I gather you know that story."

"Yes. Mr Chatham told me."

"So I said I'd give him a character reference if that would help. But he went very fierce and said no, modelling was degrading, he didn't want anyone to know he'd done it. I imagine that was why he'd had his hair vandalised at that place I always send them to in Hanover Square. He was afraid of being recognised from the ads. He's a very complicated young man."

"So I've discovered."

"Anyway, it turned out he'd fixed himself up with a job."

"You don't know where?"

"No. Wait, though, I think he said one of the girls knew of a nursery garden that wanted extra hands, and she'd talked to the proprietor."

"Oh," said Celia. "I wonder, could that by any chance have been Hodson's Garden Centre, quite near here on the London road from Haxton?"

There was a stunned silence at the other end.

"My God, I never thought of that," said Sandra Morrison and broke into throaty gurgles of laughter.

"Do explain the joke," Celia asked coldly as the laughter got louder.

"I'm sorry, it would take ages to explain, it's too complicated."

"But you think that's where this girl found him a job?"

"Probably, yes, but will you excuse me now? There's someone on the other line."

Damn the woman, why couldn't she explain? It was probably a dim advertising joke, not really funny at all. But it was frustrating not to know, Celia's unhappiness-factor was high enough already and this was the last straw. That infuriating laughter must mean something. She was obsessed by it, as if it was the key to the whole messy riddle, and at the same time annoyed with herself for worrying about anything so footling.

While she was in the village shop posting off her plant orders the postman saved himself a journey by handing her her mail. It included the private detective's report on the travels of Bert Hodson's white van. A discreet yard near King's Cross station, she read . . . and began to laugh. But only at relief over a problem solved. Sandra Morrison's joke was not really very funny but the mental fog had lifted leaving the answer clear to see. She knew now why the van had blind sides and a ventilator on top, what the "meetings" in the Manor House were about, why Hodson wanted a back entrance.

Feeling slightly better pleased with life she drove back to Archerscroft, but as she turned in from the lane Bill came hurtling out on his motorcycle. They almost collided. Bill put his feet down and tried to heave the bike past the van. What could be seen of his face through the perspex of his helmet was scarlet. Goodness, thought Celia, the famous temper had erupted.

"Hey, where are you off to?"

"I'm leaving. I'll not be called a thief," he shouted, and revved the bike furiously.

"Whoa! Steady, who says you are?"

"You do. You think I stole your primroses. Mrs Hallam told me."

"I said nothing of the kind, she's a mad gossiping busybody," Celia yelled over the noise of his engine.

"But you did think that."

Since this was true, she decided on shock treatment. "Who d'you think I am? Richard Chatham?"

Behind the perspex, his jaw dropped.

"Make that thing stop its noise, I'm tired of yelling," she ordered.

He cut the engine. "You've been spying on me."

"Why not, you fed me a lot of lies. We're quits."

"Whatever that bugger Chatham told you, it's wrong."

"Don't be too sure, he's got a guilty conscience about you."

"So he damn well should have."

"Look, let me tell you what I've found out and we'll compare notes."

"I bet it's all wrong."

"You were trained at Fontbury House under a gardener called Scobie. You invented The Grange at Rugeley because you were afraid I'd check on you with Richard Chatham and be told he'd sacked you for stealing."

"I never stole nothing off him."

"I know you didn't, he confessed that he'd made that story up, and he explained why. When you left Fontbury you worked for the Sandra Morrison agency hating every minute of it and I gather saving every penny you could so that you could start up a gardening business."

"That's right, Celia, when I got more experience."

"When you left, you had a problem about references, so you asked around for jobs in gardening where you wouldn't need one. And one of the girls in the agency put you on to Hodson's."

"Nasty little cow."

"Yes. She's one of the girls who come down in the white van, isn't she?"

He nodded. "Getting me a job there was her idea of a funny funny joke."

No doubt it had seemed comic to her, and to Sandra Morrison, that the straitlaced Bill Wilkins should leave modelling to work at a garden centre which was a front for what the French call a House of Tolerance and the British in their more censorious moods a House of Ill Repute.

98

NINE

"How did you find out it was that?" Bill asked.

"I got a detective agency to follow the van that the girls travel in."

According to the agency's report the white van's base was an unobtrusive yard near King's Cross station in London. The girls embarked there in the morning and were taken down to the garden centre. At the end of their labours the van took them back to London. But how did they get from the shed with the electrically operated door to the Old Manor House?

"There's a passage underground," Bill explained. "It starts from an inspection pit in the floor of the shed, like they have in garages."

These elaborate precautions were wise, Celia thought. In a big city it was easy to slip into a discreet doorway offering massage, but such comings and goings would attract attention at once in a town the size of Haxton, unless they took place under cover of a crowd of people going about their legitimate business. This was what Bert Hodson had provided. The Old Manor House was on a busy main road. It could do a roaring trade, but only if it kept the secret of what it was.

Bill had wheeled his bike back into the yard and propped it on its stand. When he took off his helmet a gruesome sight was unveiled. The whole left side of his neck was a raw, livid bruise. A jagged cut with five stitches in it ran from just below his ear to the base of his throat.

"Goodness, Bill. What have you been up to?"

"I got in a fight." He took off the leather jacket, revealing a

99

bandaged forearm. "That's why I was late, on account of being sewn up at the hospital."

"Oh Bill, must you fight people?"

"It wasn't me started it. Two of Hodson's men was waiting for me when I went to get out the bike."

"It would be them. Why?"

"Old Mr Hodson don't like me, on account of me hitting him."

Hodson, misled by the girl who had recommended Bill, had assumed that he would be willing to help out in the Old Manor House as well as at the garden centre. He had taken Bill in there and had proposed a course of action involving a girl and an "old geezer" which astonished and disgusted him. When he refused, point blank, there had been "a lot of effing and beeing and nasty words" from Hodson, till Bill shut him up by hitting him on the nose.

"You must learn to say 'no' without hitting people," Celia urged. "Women have to do it all the time."

Having bloodied Hodson he walked out and spent a week looking in vain for a job where he would get good horticultural experience. He was delighted when Celia took him on.

"But you did think I stole your primroses," he said, frowning.

"To be honest, I wondered about them when you didn't turn up. I thought you'd been sent by Bert Hodson to steal them."

This bewildered him and she had to explain about her dealings with Hodson. "He's trying to buy me out. During the day the Old Manor House customers can drop in at the garden centre and nobody notices, that takes care of the lunchtime passing trade. But the garden centre closes at six, which is when businessmen can "lose" an hour or so on their way home. If he had a discreet back entrance he could keep open after the garden centre shuts. That's why he's bullying me to sell. Last time he was here he almost threatened to steal those primroses, and he has."

"That's naughty, you should get them back off of him."

"Yes, I shall attend to that now. But shouldn't you go home?"

He refused flatly to take the day off and nurse his injuries. "I'm okay. Lucky I had my helmet on or I'd have been hurt worse. How d'you plan to grab back them primroses?"

"Well, I shall have to climb a tree for the first time since I was a girl. D'you feel fit enough to give me a leg up?"

He nodded. "I'll stiffen up less if I keep moving. What d'you want with climbing trees then?"

When she explained her plan he laughed till his neck began to hurt. They made their preparations quickly and set off through the coppice and rough pasture which lay between Archerscroft and Hodson's garden centre. Near the far side of it was a fine wide-branching holm oak. By alternate pushing at her backside and pulling on her arms from above, Bill got her up into it. They installed themselves side by side on a high branch which commanded a good view over the garden centre, and hid them with its foliage.

"That's a good camera you have there," said Bill, with knowledge born from much time spent as lens-fodder.

"Yes, it belonged to my husband," said Celia, screwing in the telephoto lens and preparing to snap the furtive comings and goings at the side door of the Old Manor House. Bill, armed with field glasses, stood by to act as spotter.

"Here comes one," he reported. "Going up to the door very very casual, but wait, he's got his back to us. Bet he looks round though, to see if anyone's watching . . . yes, now!"

"Goodness," said Celia, as she snapped him twice, "that was the Chairman of the Borough Finance Committee."

After a longish wait two more men went in, but without presenting themselves in full face or profile.

"We'll have to wait till they come out," said Celia. "I imagine you disapprove of brothels?"

He considered. "I dunno what I think, why d'you say that?"

"I gather you're against casual sex."

"For myself, I am. I'm against people who take a look at me and say, 'I'll have that,' as if I was a thing and not a person."

Celia was going to say, "Now you know what the feminists are on about," but the need to photograph Haxton's leading

101

solicitor interrupted her. He was followed by Timothy Foster.

"Oh good," said Celia. "I was hoping to bag him."

"I've never been as happy as I was at Fontbury," Bill went on, following his own train of thought. "Then Mr Chatham lost control of himself and gave me a bad name to get out of his scrape and I had to leave. That's only the first time, there's women as well as men that made aggro for me. People go mad when you won't do what they want. Most of the time sex is a pain in the neck all round."

Celia bagged two senior accountants and a prosperous farmer. "But Bill, you mustn't let your troubles put you off girls altogether."

What she thought of as his pretty-boy sulk reappeared. She realised now that it expressed embarrassment. "You're getting me wrong, I'm not against it when two people are serious about each other, it's lovely. Me and my girl were together six months in London before her family broke it up."

"What happened to her?" Celia asked.

"Her father said I was rubbish and took her off on a world cruise. I was rubbish too, poncing around as a male beauty queen. When I get me own gardening business, maybe he'll think different."

He lapsed into grim silence. Two more local personalities fell victim to the telephoto lens, together with a mixed bag of unidentified small fry. Celia decided to call it a day and unscrewed the lens.

"I bet you get your primroses back okay," said Bill, cheering up. "When he sees what you got in there he'll offer you half the nursery stock to go away and keep quiet."

"Now, Mr Hodson," said Celia, spreading out her photos on his desk. "The negatives are at my bank, just in case of accidents. Unless I get satisfaction now, prints will be posted off this evening to the wives of all these people, to the *Haxton Gazette*, and to every women's organisation in the district."

Hodson was still leaning back in his chair, apparently at ease.

"Had some plants pilfered, did you? O deary me, it's always happening, the public has no conscience these days. Those lovely primroses, did you say, what we was admiring the other morning?"

"Yes."

He leant forward with an expression of patient concern for the weak-minded. "But they're not here, dear. You've not been yourself lately. I hear very sad stories about you in the village. It's just one of your delusions, you thinking I've stole your primroses. Now you go home and look round, you'll find you put them somewhere and forgot."

Celia rose and gathered up the prints. "If you say my primroses aren't here there's no point in my hanging on to these, I may as well post them off. There'll be a scandal of course and the police will be forced to take notice and close you down, so warn all your customers to expect trouble."

He let her get halfway to the door. "Miz Grant, one moment."

"Yes?"

"I'm always happy to help out a colleague what's down on their luck. Suppose I said I'd replace the stock you lost with something very similar."

"How similar?"

"You'd never tell the difference," said Hodson, winking genially. "And in return you'd agree not to embarrass my distinguished clientele, eh?"

"We'll talk about that when I've seen the primroses."

He stalled for a little longer before he went out of the room to murmur an instruction to a henchman. Ten minutes later Celia was inspecting her primroses, which had materialised in the back of her van.

"All present and correct?" Hodson asked.

All twelve were there. Three more were showing colour.

"Swop them for that negative, eh?" Hodson suggested.

"Oh no, Mr Hodson. I'll feel safer with it in my bank, just in case you felt tempted not to leave me and Mr Wilkins in peace in future. Good afternoon."

On the drive back to Archerscroft she reviewed progress and was alarmed to discover that the list of unanswered questions was getting longer and longer. To start with, Bill Wilkins had not been planted on her by her enemies, therefore Deirdre Foster had not been got out of the way to make room for him. Where then was Deirdre, and why had she been taken smartly out of circulation? Why had her husband lied about her mother's broken leg? What was Timothy Foster's connection with Bert Hodson? Professional, as the estate agent handling the sale of some land Hodson wanted to buy, and commercial as a customer at the Old Manor House, but what else? He seemed to have a very guilty conscience.

Another thought, very perplexing, what connection was there between the Bert Hodson carry-on and Kenny Cooper's murder? None, as far as she could see, except that Timothy Foster, via his wife, was one of the first people to be warned that the herbaceous border at The Towers was under suspicion of containing something unusual. He could have passed the information on to his crony Hodson, but why would Hodson want to murder the Emersons and Kenny Cooper? Why would anyone want to?

The family at The Towers had had early warning too, and the herbaceous border was in their garden. Would one bury a body in one's own garden? Only if there was no choice, one would look first for a safer alternative elsewhere. The argument cut both ways. The herbaceous border could have been the Armitages' only choice, or somebody else's safer alternative.

These were things one could theorise endlessly about. But there was another urgent query which had a factual answer hidden somewhere, it was a matter of beavering away till one found it: why had the name of Richard Chatham had such a shattering effect on Alison Fitzgerald?

She parked the van and went into the frame yard. There, potting up rooted cuttings of *Aster frikartii*, was someone who might know.

"Bill when you were at Fontbury, did you hear anyone talking about Alison Fitzgerald?"

"Who's she?"

Here was something she had been too busy to attend to till now. Far from being an undercover agent from the enemy camp, fully briefed on her predicament and under orders to make it worse, Bill knew nothing about the Emersons' murder, Kenny Cooper and everything that had happened to make Celia's name mud in the village. He must be told, before he heard a hotted up version of the story from Mrs Hallam. He listened quietly, asked a few questions, and did not seem unduly put out.

". . . so you'd better realise," she added, "that you're working for the most unpopular woman in the village, who is widely thought to be mad."

"I don't think you're mad, Celia. Gardeners are taught to observe, they look at things properly, they notice things when others don't. If you say you saw Kenny Cooper's foot, then it was there."

This was comforting. But he was as baffled as she was by the mysterious link between Fontbury and The Towers.

"This Alison. You say she dropped a trayful of tea things."

"Yes. There must be some deep-seated connection with Fontbury, but Richard Chatham seemed genuinely puzzled when I asked. He could have been lying, but I don't think so, he told me the truth about you."

"She's hysterical, you said. It could have been something else set her off. She sees she's forgot to put any milk in the jug, so she's cross with herself and has a fit."

"No, it must have been more than that, Nigel and Boxie were terrified of what she'd say next."

They cudgelled their brains for a time without results.

"Okay, I'll tell you what we do," Bill suggested. "We go up to that garden with the little Japanese bridges and we cut the grass and we tidy it up nice. We work hard and we sweat like pigs and after that we settle down and we'll think. Old Scobie at Fontbury gave me that advice, when you've got a problem, he said, you do an hour's double trenching, everything will surely look clearer after a good sweat."

But several hours' exercise brought them no nearer to solving

105

the problem. They returned to Archerscroft and attacked it again over mugs of tea.

"Old Scobie gave me another piece of advice. When you've mislaid a tool in the garden, he said, think back over everything you did and you'll find it."

The relevance of this was not obvious to Celia.

"Maybe if you think back over everything that happened when you was in there, before she dropped the tray. Then perhaps you'll remember something you forgot."

Celia shut her eyes and concentrated.

"Start from when the old girl, Boxie is that her name? When she let you into the house."

"Alison and Nellie had quarrelled, I think. Alison didn't want me to come in, but Nellie insisted that I should, to spite her . . ." She went right through the whole scene in detail, to the moment of climax. ". . . And Nellie was trying to remember Richard Chatham's name and couldn't. Then she did and crash, the tea was on the floor and Alison was having hysterics. It must have been that."

"Maybe, maybe not. Where was Alison standing? In the doorway?"

"No, she was right beside me, waiting to put the tray down when I'd cleared the table."

"What was on it that had to be cleared?"

"Books."

"Nothing else?"

"Oh. Yes. One of Nellie's flower paintings was under the pile of books. I made some remark about it, but that was the moment when Nellie remembered Richard Chatham's name."

"Then Alison sees this painting, she must have done. She's looking to see if the table's clear so she can put down the tray. How long before she starts screaming?"

"Almost at once. Before Nellie had stopped speaking."

"Then there you are, it was the painting," said Bill.

"No, I'm not. Alison's seen thousands of Nellie's flower pictures, why should this one make her scream?"

106

"I dunno."

"Wait, I've had an idea," said Celia. "It was horribly hot in Nellie's room, they'd had a fire in there. I remember wondering why they wanted one, it was quite warm outside."

"Had they been burning something then?"

"Yes. It could have been paper in the grate, I didn't notice. Suppose they'd been burning a whole lot of Nellie's drawings . . ."

"Why?"

"I've no idea, but let's suppose. I lift up the books on the table, and there is this drawing that I'm not supposed to see, goodness knows why, but I'm not. Alison sees for the first time that it's been overlooked and not burnt with the others so she screams."

This still left unsolved the question of why Nellie's paintings had to be burnt.

"But suppose that's what they quarrelled about?" Celia suggested. "Nellie didn't want them burnt, but Alison insisted."

"What flower was it in the picture you saw?" Bill asked.

"A nasturtium. Not the ordinary one with the orange flower. Alison started her performance with the tray, or I'd have asked Nellie what it was."

"They have lots of varieties besides the orange."

"I know, but I don't think it was one, it was a deep yellow and the three lower petals were heavily bearded, with a dark red bar right down the middle. I've never seen that, have you? Let's look it up."

After a moment's hesitation she led the way up the stairs and unlocked the oak door at the top. "I keep my husband's horticultural library up here out of the way of burglars because some of the books are valuable. As you see, this is my bedroom but let's get one thing clear. I'm old enough to be your mother and have no intention of being hit on the nose."

He grinned. "I'm not worried, I know you're okay."

"What d'you mean, okay?"

"There's women a lot older than you that would have their fingers in my hair as soon as look at me, but I've got so I can tell who's okay and who isn't."

"Well, your hair's quite safe from me, so pass me the Royal Horticultural Society's *Dictionary of Gardening*. No, the second volume, it will be under 'T'."

"Nasturtium's under 'N'," he objected.

"But it'll be under the Latin name, which is *Tropaeolum*."

"You'd think nasturtium would be the Latin name for nasturtium," he grumbled.

"No, when it first arrived in Europe the herbalists wondered what it would cure people of, which was all they cared about, and they tasted it and decided it tasted a bit like cress. So they classified it quite wrongly as a nasturtium, which is the Latin name for the cress family and the name stuck. . . . Here we are, *Tropaeolum*, goodness I had no idea there were so many. *Peregrinum*, that's the Canary Creeper, but I don't see anything like Nellie's flower here except . . . ah yes, *Tropaeolum minus*. Flowers deep yellow, yes. Petals ending in a bristle-like point, yes, I think they were a bit pointed. Lower petals much spotted, but what colour are the spots, why can't they say? It was brought to Europe from Peru, that would be by the Spaniards who conquered it, and it was growing in a botanical garden in Genoa in about 1585. Nellie's plant could be *Tropaeolum minus*, but those spots worry me, it was more like a bar and I wish I knew what colour. Can you get me down that big leather-bound book at the end of the top shelf?"

He reached down Gerard's *Herbal* and handed it to her. "Now. Gerard was a herbalist and he treated it as a cress. Let's look up cress in the index. Here we are, Indian cress, page 251."

"It's all spelt funny," Bill complained, reading over her shoulder.

"Everybody spelt funny in 1633," said Celia, and began to look down the entry.

Creſſes of India haue many weake and feeble branches, riſing immediately from the grovnd, diſperſing themselves far abroade; by means whereof one plant doth occvpie a great circvit of grovnd, as doth the Greate Bindeweede.

"Yes yes, we know all about that," said Celia. "Let's see what he says about the flower."

> The flowers are difperfed throughout the whole plant, of colour yellow, with a croffed ftar ouerthwart the infide, of a deep orange colour.

The illustration was a crude woodcut in black and white.

"I don't like the sound of 'deep orange'," Celia muttered. "Nellie's was definitely crimson. But Gerard was an awful old fraud, he copied a lot from other people, he may not even have seen the plant in flower."

"He says what the seed's like," Bill pointed out. "Wasn't there no seed or seed-case in Nellie's picture?"

"No, it wasn't a botanical drawing, more like a study with sketches of four or five flowerheads. Reach me down Parkinson* from up there, will you? He's a bit better on flowers, let's try him. . . . Oh bother, another horrid woodcut that doesn't tell one anything, but what about the text? Here we are, the flowers are of 'an excellent gold colour'. He talks about 'leaves' when he means petals but never mind. Oh goody, goody, what did I tell you?

> In the middle of eache of the three lower leaues (yet fometimes it is bvt in two of them) there is a long fpot or ftreake of an excellent crimfon colour, with a long heele or fpur behind hanging downe. The whole flower hath a nice fmall fent, which being placed in the middle of fome carnations or Gilloflowers make a delicate tuffiemuffie, as they call it, or nofegay.

"So there's our crimson bar," Celia gloated. "And he says the flower 'is of great beauty and sweetness withall, that any garden of delight cannot be unfurnished with it.' That must mean it was quite common in the seventeenth century."

"Why did they stop having it, then?" Bill asked.

"I think I can guess. Let's look at the *Dictionary of Gardening*

*Parkinson, *Paradisi in Sole Paradisus Terrestris*, or The Garden of Pleasant Flowers, London 1629.

again. Here's the answer. The big orange nasturtium that everyone has was introduced here in 1686. The flowers are much bigger and it's much showier and it produced interesting colour variations, so people started cultivating that instead."

"Your one sounds nice, though. I've never seen it."

Suddenly Celia's brain gave a great heave, and threw up a memory from the past. "I know where one can see it."

"Where?"

"Miles away. In Derbyshire."

Celia tapped Bill on the shoulder and shouted in his ear, "Here's our exit." He slowed down to ninety, then eighty, then seventy, ready to leave the motorway. She had been terrified at first, shutting her eyes and wishing she was dead. But once she had learnt to lean with the bike instead of fighting it she began to feel pleased with life, like a Greek nymph cadging a lift on a very vivacious dolphin. It was only eleven and they were almost there. She was enormously grateful to Bill; slogging up to Derbyshire and back in the pick-up would have taken hours longer.

He swung off the motorway and threaded through heavy traffic till their route left the main road and headed up a winding river valley with overhanging trees. Presently the valley broadened out into water meadows and there, perched above them against its background of beechwoods, was Melsingham, an astonishing outburst of architecture which looked as if the National Gallery had transferred itself from Trafalgar Square to get away from the traffic.

The great gates were open. Beside them was a notice giving times and prices of admission. Melsingham, like every other house of its size, was struggling grimly for survival and the car park was full of coaches, ice cream stalls and notices directing customers to children's paddling pools, souvenir shops, zoos, donkey rides and all the other moneymaking attractions with which houses in this predicament surround themselves.

Feeling rather strange in her borrowed motorcycling gear, Celia went into the grand marble entrance hall and bought them two tickets.

"It's in the house, then, not in the garden?" Bill asked.

She remembered clearly the small room it was in. It was only four years since she and Roger stayed at Melsingham while he advised on the rescue of an overgrown Georgian fern grotto.

"There you are," she said. "*Tropaeolum minus*, alias Indian Cress."

The picture was tiny, a Dutch flower piece barely ten inches high. Each flower in the bouquet was a highly finished portrait with nothing fudged or blurred; irises, roses, a carnation, some small cyclamens, a snowflake and as top flower a striped, strangely elongated tulip. There were two *Tropaeolum minus* blooms, one of them half hidden behind the stem of the tulip. According to the label on the frame the painter was one C. van den Berghe.*

"That's not natural, the seasons are all wrong," Bill objected. "You'd never get irises and roses and the cyclamens and nasturtiums and that snowflake thing to put in a vase at the same time."

"Oh, but that's not the way a Dutch flower painter operated. If he stuffed flowers in a vase and started to paint they'd be dead before he'd finished his first tulip. He'd have a stock of studies of different flowers on separate pieces of paper and when he had a commission he'd paint the vase and copy his studies into it one by one till he'd got a bouquet. You sometimes see the same flower, a narcissus with a twisted petal or a rose with a curving stem, turn up in picture after picture by the same artist."

They looked at the stiff little bouquet for a long time.

*Christoffel van den Berghe (c. 1590-c. 1642) worked in Middelburg. He often depicted unusual flowers, including the *Tropaeolum*, which do not appear in the work of other Dutch flower painters. See L.J. Bol, *Holländische Maler des 17 Jahrhunderts nahe den grossen Meistern*, Brunswick, 1969. The picture described above was in the Hildebrand sale in Berlin in 1912, after which its whereabouts were unknown for a time; it was rediscovered at Melsingham by the present writer.

"That nasturtium of the old lady's," said Bill. "It wasn't no botanical drawing, you said."

"No, it was a study, that's why I had to come here and check. There were four or five flower heads in it, and I'm sure two of them were copies from the two in this picture."

"Why would she want to do that?"

"There could be all sorts of reasons. The real question is, why did Alison panic when she saw Nellie's effort lying right under my nose?"

"She knew you're clever at flowers. You'd say, 'that's a funny nasturtium,' and look for it in them books of yours. But why wouldn't she want you to? I dunno."

"Remember, her nerves are all anyhow, she's panicking at very remote dangers all the time. I think she was afraid I'd find out somehow that Nellie had copied her nasturtiums from this picture."

"Is it wrong to copy off a picture then?"

"Only if you do it for dishonest reasons. If you were a forger and wanted to fake a picture by Christoffel van den Berghe, how would you start?"

"I'd copy the flowers off a real picture by him, like the studies the old painters had, so you could put them together different. And everyone would say, 'look at those nasturtiums, it must be by that Van den Berghe.'"

"Exactly."

"Cor, naughty old Nellie."

TEN

"SORRY, NO," THE girl on the bookstall told Celia, but she was gazing raptly at Bill. It was the first time Celia had seen the unsettling effect he produced on young women and the scowl of disdain which their unseemly behaviour produced in Bill.

"Not even a postcard?" Celia insisted. It was important to establish this. If reproductions of the Van den Berghe were not available, Nellie must have come to Melsingham herself to make studies from it.

"Sorry, no," the girl repeated loudly as if to the deaf.

"I wonder if it's been reproduced in some book?"

"I told you," said the girl, becoming really stroppy, "we've no reproduction of that picture on sale here."

"But that wasn't what I asked you."

"Silly cow," Bill commented without lowering his voice excessively. "Isn't there no one sensible we can ask?"

"Yes, Hermione and Everard will know, but I thought we'd check here first. Come along, it's through here."

Ignoring shrewish cries from the bookstall of "where d'you think you're going?" she slipped round behind it and through a door marked "Private" into a gloomy stone-flagged passage.

"There's an office somewhere down here with a secretary . . . yes, here we are. Hullo, Miss Moffat, how are you? Is either of them in?"

"I'll ask. Mrs Grant, isn't it? How nice to see you again." Miss Moffat buzzed the house telephone. "Your grace? Mrs Roger Grant is here."

The house telephone squawked with pleasure.

"She says, will you go along," Miss Moffat reported. "You know the way, don't you?"

Followed by Bill, Celia went on down the stone-flagged passage. A door at the end opened and a woman with an elegant figure and unremarkable clothes cried, "Celia dear, how nice."

"Hullo, Hermione. Sorry to barge in like this."

"Nonsense dear, it's a treat to see you. But why are you dressed like that, not fascist rallies I hope?"

"No, motorcycling. Bill here whisked me up the motorway behind him like a Valkyrie on a fire-horse. My car's far too slow."

"You'll stay to lunch?" She shouted down the passage. "Moffat dear, will you please tell them we'll be two extra?"

"Very well, your grace."

Bill switched on his embarrassment-sulk, thought better of it and substituted a beautiful smile. "It's kind of you, ma'am, but I belong in the servants' quarters."

"Oh piffle," said the duchess. "These are the servants' quarters, the rest of the house is full of paying customers. Anyway servants are an extinct species so you'll have to pig it with us, won't he, Celia? Come on in."

Her sitting room was pleasantly shabby and full of teenage offspring and small yapping dogs.

"Everard's at a grand do in Derby for the Prince of Wales," the duchess explained, pouring out drinks. "But I'll murder him if he's not back in time to rod out the drains this afternoon. There's a very sinister puddle behind the male visitors' loo."

The two boys had taken charge of Bill, and were talking motorcycles. The eldest girl was paralysed with admiration for his profile.

"He's enchanting dear, but what's wrong with his neck?" muttered the duchess. "All those stitches—have you been biting it?"

"No, our relations are very chaste. I hired him to help me garden but he got into a fight. I seem to have developed into a Miss Marple and he's become my Watson and I crept around in my mittens and

114

sniffed out an art forgery. That's why I'm here, to have a look at the little Van den Berghe."

The duchess put down her glass. "What on earth is it about that picture? No one takes a blind bit of notice of the Rembrandt or the Frans Hals, all the action is about a flowerpiece the size of a beer mat by a minor Dutchman."

"What action? Who else is interested?"

"An expert called Peeters from Holland, for one. He came banging on the door last winter when we were shut, and it turned out he'd come all the way from Amsterdam to tell us it wasn't a fake, extraordinary. He was huge, six feet tall and more or less square. I've never seen a man eat so much."

"Hermione, this is very important. Please tell me all about it."

"Well, he began by saying someone had started faking flower-pieces by minor Dutch masters, which apparently is quite a sensible thing to do, because although they fetch good prices they're not going to be looked at as carefully as a Vermeer, say, it's much easier to get away with it. And then he produced what he said was a fake Van den Berghe from his briefcase and held it up beside ours, and I must say it looked quite pukka to me."

"Was it a straight copy of your picture?"

"No, about half the flowers were copied from ours and the rest, especially the tulips, from a Van den Berghe rather like ours that's in the Philadelphia Museum of Art* and they'd been put together to make quite a different bouquet."

"Had Peeters any idea who was doing the faking?"

"He seemed to think it had been done in England, probably by someone with good botanical knowledge and an art school training. He asked if we'd any suggestions. Have you?"

"Yes. You don't remember a very old lady hobbling up to your picture on two sticks and whipping out her paintbox and making studies from it? No, on second thoughts she wouldn't risk that, she must have worked from a reproduction. Are there any?"

*In the John G. Johnson Collection. It has an iris as the top flower rather than a tulip, but some of the other flowers, including a *Leucojum vernum*, are identical in both pictures, though differently arranged.

"That was the other odd thing, Celia. About a year ago a London gallery wrote and said could they send a photographer along because they were doing a coffee table book about flower paintings and wanted to include it. And we agreed and the photographer came and we were going to get a complimentary copy of the book, but it never materialised. I assumed that the book wasn't out yet, but Peeters seemed to think the whole thing was very sinister."

"Hermione dear, I beg of you: Address of Peeters. Date when he was here. Address of sinister London gallery. When was photo taken. I shall have a stroke with frustration if you've forgotten or thrown away Peeters' visiting card."

"Have no fear, we unpaid keepers of the nation's heritage have to be methodical. Help yourself to more sherry while I get Miss Moffat to look it all up."

She went, and came back quite soon with a typewritten slip of paper which she handed to Celia.

"Come along everybody, lunch," she cried. "We're going across to the orangery because we can eat there free and don't have to wash up. Everard's turned it into a snob restaurant for the expense account trade. You'll have to eat scampi and so on, things that businessmen like, I hope you don't mind?"

Celia looked at Miss Moffat's typewritten note. Dr Jan Peeters of Amsterdam had visited Melsingham a week before the Emersons were murdered.

The Omphalos Gallery, Celia read. According to Miss Moffat this was the gallery which had asked to photograph the picture at Melsingham. As Bill turned into the little side street off Berkeley Square she had half expected to find an accommodation address at a seedy newsagents, but no. Its name was in gold lettering on spick-and-span royal blue, there was an up-market Madonna and Child in the window and thanks to a virtuoso performance by Bill on the motorway it had not yet closed for the night. Inside could be discerned an elegant young man at a desk and walls covered with expensive-looking little pictures.

"You going in?" Bill asked.

"I suppose so," said Celia without a clear idea of what this would achieve. "Why don't you stay here with the bike, and prance in if I seem to be running into trouble?"

Bill studied the elegant young man. "I reckon you'll be safe enough with that creature. I'll pretend to be looking at Mary and the Baby here, so I can see if he starts being naughty."

Celia pushed open the door and went in. Seen at closer quarters the pictures on sale were of no particular school, a jumble of Dutch, Italian and French work, mostly of the eighteenth or nineteenth centuries and including a few minor items by major names. There was a marked absence of flower-pieces.

"I'm afraid we're just closing," said the young man, rising from his desk. "Was it anything in particular?"

"I'm looking for flower-pieces," said Celia, trying to sound as if she could afford one.

"There's a nice little Manet over there," he said, waving a hand towards an oil sketch of a vase containing one splurgy rose.

"Ah no, I meant one of those elaborate Dutch affairs with half the Chelsea Flower Show in them."

"I see, one moment please." He lifted the telephone. "Mrs Slansky, I have a lady here enquiring for Dutch flower-pieces."

A woman came out of a back room wearing a saleswomanly smile of welcome, which was wiped off by the shock of recognition when she saw Celia. The shock was mutual. Celia was about to say, "We've met before," when she noticed that the welcoming smile was being hoisted back into position.

"You are wantink some Dutch flower-pisses?" asked Mrs Slansky softly.

Okay, thought Celia, if you want to play "let's pretend" I'm game and I shall damn well keep you guessing whether I've recognised you or not. Her enthusiasm for Dutch flower-pieces was such that Mrs Slansky was reminded of one which was not in the shop at the moment but which was of such an exquisiteness that Celia must come back to see it.

"So, pliss, you will let me haf your name and also your telephone number."

"Oh, but I'm going out of town tomorrow, I'll ring you when I get back next week."

"Do, pliss. May I know your name?"

"Octavia Brown. Mrs," Celia lied. And if I do come back, she thought, I shall bring a cyclamen from the Old Rectory garden with me and stuff it down your throat.

On the way home Celia called a halt at a pub to eat.

"I saw the lot through the window," said Bill between mouthfuls. "First she puts on the welcome-welcome look like shop ladies do, then she sees you and thinks, 'crikey, I know her,' but she's not sure so she puts the welcome back on again."

"Or she is sure, but she puts on the welcome again because she hopes I haven't recognised her. In either case she'll warn them at The Towers that I know a lot more than they thought."

Bill nodded. "We ought to watch out, they may get naughty."

They ate for a few minutes in silence. Celia was secretly comforted by the word "we"

"Who d'you reckon's in it at The Towers?" Bill asked. "Besides Nellie?"

"Alison for one. If visitors come when Nellie's forging away upstairs Alison gets her down on that chair lift thing before the visitors are let in."

"How about Roy and Nigel? Alison's a bit mental, you said. She'd blab it out to her menfolk."

"Roy must know, he's the one she takes her troubles to. I'm not sure about Nigel."

"And Roy's missis?" he prompted.

Celia thought about this. "I doubt it. The Slansky carry-on with the cyclamen happened in Harriet's garden, but Roy could easily have organised that without telling her. She wouldn't have performed convincingly if she'd been in the know, she's hopeless at acting, her Lady Bracknell with the Village Players was embarrassing to a degree. Besides, I don't think the others treat

118

her as family, she's just a rich woman that Roy happened to marry."

"She smacks their fingers when they paw at the money bags, I bet. I had an auntie no one liked for that."

"I'm sure she keeps Roy short. He seems to depend on what he wins on horses."

"Oh Celia, no one can live off the horses. The horses live off the people. So Nellie has to sweat away at her forging to keep the others from going on the supplementary benefit?"

"That could well be. I don't know how much old Sir Henry left, but plant collecting's not a gold mine. Nor is sculpture, and according to Nellie Alison hasn't any money."

"I bet you Nigel's in it along with Roy. You'd need two to grub up that body double-quick and hide it. And there's the haystack needed setting fire to."

"Yes," said Celia. "The haystack was Nigel's style. He'd notice a way of getting all the village phones cut off, and store the idea for future reference."

"Maybe they sent Alison. You don't need no brains to fire a haystack."

"She might not have the guts, but aren't we going too fast? Because Nellie's a forger it doesn't prove that the Armitage family killed Kenny Cooper and chopped up the Emersons with an axe. Why would they want to?"

"Say the Emersons spotted Nellie's naughty game?"

"How would they, Bill? They both worked in London, he was an accountant and she ran a hairdressing business. Besides, how does Kenny fit in?"

"Nigel used to send for him to help with his funny-funny tricks, right? And it was a secret, right? No one knew Kenny was coming to The Towers to see Nigel?"

"Yes, but where does that get us?"

"When they've finished killing the Emersons Nigel phones Kenny to come as usual, and they chop him too and bury him, so everyone will think that wicked delinquent boy did that shocking brutal crime and what a disgrace to our village."

119

"Which is exactly what they did say, I admit, with Harriet leading the chorus."

"Then she's in it too, after all."

"It doesn't follow. Roy could have put her up to it without telling her why, she's very stupid. But oh dear, isn't all this far too bloodthirsty? They don't shut you up for life for forging pictures, nothing disastrous happened to that man with the phoney Samuel Palmers. Three murders just to cover up a bit of picture-faking? Surely not."

"I dunno, but these are nasty people. Look what they did to you."

He went to fetch coffee from the bar. When he came back he was looking grim. "I've been thinking. That gallery woman's going to tip them off that you know more than they think, going in and asking for Dutch pictures and all, and they'll get very naughty. So when we get to your place you're letting me go in first."

Celia called for the bill. "But you're only supposed to help me garden, I've no right to treat you as a bodyguard."

"You have, Celia," he said, as his face settled into the embarrassment-sulk. "You have every right. You took a chance on me, I was at four places first and they looked at me like I was a dog's mess and said, 'where's your references?' You gave me a break."

Celia had taken him on partly because she was highly suspicious of him, and partly because she was desperate for anyone capable of walking behind a lawnmower. But this was not the moment to say so.

"I'm not sure why I took you on, but I'm very glad I did. And to be honest, I was dreading going into the cottage alone, so offer accepted with grateful thanks."

When Bill turned into the gate at Archerscroft and cut his engine she was even more grateful. The night was like ink and she was shivering from the rush through the night air. He went in and switched on the lights. Presently, when nothing alarming had happened, she stepped into the hall.

120

"Did you lock the back door when we went?" Bill called from the kitchen.

"Yes, and bolted it. I remember distinctly."

"You're sure? It's not locked now."

"Then someone's been."

"How did they get in then?" Bill asked, and began going round the windows.

Celia nerved herself and opened the sitting room curtains, hoping nothing sinister was behind them. "Here," she said. The catch on the French window had been forced.

"Penknife," Bill decided. "Anything been stolen?"

"Not that I can see. Would there be?"

"If it was just kids breaking in. It's not. No mess."

"Bill. They could still be upstairs."

But the oak door at the top of the stairs was locked and the key was in its usual daytime hiding-place. Bill unlocked the door and searched the bedrooms but found nothing. He came down again and stood frowning at the French window.

"That back door, it's not right somehow. You'd think they'd go out this way, like when they came in."

"Yes. Why was it unlocked? If they'd left it we might not have noticed they'd been."

Bill fetched a big electric torch. "I'll just have a look round outside, okay?"

"Bless you, Bill. Tea, if I make some?"

"Fine. I'll not be long."

But he was away some minutes. She was carrying a tray of tea into the sitting room when he came running back, looking shocked. "Don't touch that milk, Celia. Pour it away. Pour away everything that's to drink in the house unless it's in a sealed can or bottle."

"Goodness, Bill. Why?"

"You come and see."

The padlock on the potting shed door had gone. Bill shone his torch inside. There was a wine bottle on the bench and a shattered teacup on the floor.

"Remember that Paraquat concentrate you had in the toolshed?" he said. "The can's gone. The wine bottle's half-full of something, and I think I know what."

Celia shut her eyes, feeling very ill. A pupil of Roger's had once drunk a few drops of Paraquat by mistake. His death was agonised and not very quick.*

But it was the insult as well as the cruelty. Already she was the crazy woman who had delusions about bodies in flowerbeds and accused respectable people of stealing plants. Now she was to be the secret tippler out of teacups who forgot that she had been lunatic enough to put Paraquat into a wine bottle without even labelling it.

"Wait though, Bill. They couldn't have expected me to come out here and have a swig."

"That's why they unlocked the back door."

"Oh God, let me get this straight. When I'm found, I'm either dead or with my throat and lungs too far gone to speak. They see the bottle and the broken teacup and they decide that I've rushed in to the house to telephone or wash my mouth out or something."

"That's right."

"But what's really happened is, I've drunk some Paraquat that's in the house already."

"The milk, most likely. They'd reckon on you making a cup of tea or coffee or perhaps having a whisky before you go to bed. You better pour away everything like I said."

I must not cry in front of Bill, Celia repeated to herself over and over again as she poured milk and whisky and sherry and orange juice down the sink. But she longed for a really loud wail.

"It's nearly one o'clock," she told him. "You go off home, I'll be all right."

But I am a liar, she thought, I shall not be all right.

*Warning to would-be poisoners: Paraquat is no longer available as a colourless and odourless liquid, but is marketed with additives to give it a warning colour, an offensive smell and an immediate emetic effect. One must suppose that Celia used chemicals sparingly and that the can contained old stock.

"I'm not leaving you here alone, that sofa thing'll do for me."

"Oh Bill, would you? There's another bedroom upstairs, much more comfortable than the sofa. Tomorrow is one of Mrs Hallam's days though. Finding you here will over-excite her."

"Damn Mrs Hallam, I don't care what she says."

"Nor do I if you don't. According to the present buzz I'm a lesbian, I suppose having a lover half my age is a step up from that."

"Your village is full of nasty people."

"I know. There's a sealed bottle of whisky here. Let's open it and drink to them rotting in hell."

But halfway through pouring the drinks an idea hit her. "Bill, I'm a fool. Someone must be watching outside. If I'd died they were going to come in and take away the milk or the whisky or whatever it was and make sure the back door was open and so on."

"That's right, Celia. We should have thought of that."

"But did we lock the potting shed?"

"There's no padlock. They took it."

"I've just realised. We've poured away all the drink in the house that could be evidence. If they take away the wine bottle and the teacup I'll have no proof, I can't go to the police. I'd be mad Mrs Grant, who now claims that she's being poisoned on top of everything else."

Bill picked up the electric torch, ready to go and look.

"On second thoughts don't bother," she said. "The police would probably say I'd put the wine bottle and the teacup there myself."

Nevertheless he went to look. "Someone's making a very thorough job of this," he reported.

The shattered teacup and the wine bottle had gone.

ELEVEN

CELIA STARED UP into the darkness and tried not to get uptight about lying awake in the small hours. What tired one out was not insomnia but getting indignant about it. Besides, insomnia was a fleabite compared with her other worries. She had narrowly escaped death by poisoning and making a fuss about that at Haxton police station would merely be further evidence of her unbalanced mind. Escaping from one death-trap was not enough, she would have to do it again and again until she found the answer to the puzzle *and proved it*, with a flat-footed step-by-step proof that would make sense in a policeman's notebook.

Like a chess player studying a problem from all angles she moved the pieces about mentally on the board: Kenny Cooper, the Armitage family, Jan Peeters of Amsterdam, the Emersons and—yes, she was leaving someone out. Deirdre Foster.

At first Deirdre's place on the board had seemed obvious. She was the pawn that had to be removed to leave her square free for Bill Wilkins to occupy. But that theory had collapsed. Bill Wilkins, like the flowers in spring, had nothing to do with the case. Why then had Deirdre been taken out of circulation the moment the herbaceous border at The Towers came under suspicion?

"She may know something?" Bill suggested when they discussed this over breakfast.

"It could be that," said Celia. "Or perhaps they didn't want me to have a witness standing about all the time. If two people keep seeing the same things it's difficult to say one of them is having hallucinations."

"D'you think her husband knows where she is?"

"Yes. I know what I'll do, I'll frighten silly fat Timothy into telling me."

"Want me to come too, Celia? You and me together, we could frighten the dandruff out of his hair."

On reflection this seemed a very good idea. "But I feel I'm exploiting you."

"Listen Celia, it's not safe you going around alone. I'm coming everywhere with you till we sort this lot out."

"But I'm embarrassed. I pay you so little."

"I tell you what we'll do. I'll fetch my toiletries from Haxton and kip down here. You give me my board and lodging and pay me my basic, and I won't clock up no overtime, okay?"

"Even that's very generous of you, but it will electrify the village."

"Who cares what people with minds like pig bins think?" Bill asked as Mrs Hallam came bustling in to begin work.

"Oh good morning Mrs Hallam," said Celia. "Will you start by turning out the guest bedroom? Mr Wilkins is moving in there."

Mrs Hallam leered strangely with her head on one side, like a dog which has found something deliciously nasty to roll in.

"And you can spread it round the village, Mrs Hallam, that Mr Wilkins is a woman in disguise and I am passionately in love with her."

"Hee hee," shrieked Mrs Hallam unabashed, and got out the brooms.

Two hours later Celia and Bill were in the outer office of Ringmere and Foster, land agents. "Mr Foster will see you now, Mrs Grant," said the receptionist.

"Ah, come in Celia," said Timothy Foster, then caught sight of Bill.

"Mr Wilkins is my new business partner," said Celia. "As Deirdre seems to have resigned without telling me."

Timothy smiled uneasily and waved her to a chair. Bill stood in front of the desk, looking very large and solid.

"Now," said Timothy. "You've had second thoughts, you say, about Bert Hodson's offer to buy your cottage and land?"

125

"No," said Celia.

"But that's what I understood on the phone. You wanted my advice."

"I said so, yes. You'd have refused to see me if I told you why I've really come." Timothy looked at her, then at Bill, who was balancing athletically on the balls of his feet. "Celia, eccentricity is all very well, but . . ."

"I want to know where Deirdre is," Celia interrupted calmly. "And I shall sit here till you tell me."

Timothy exploded into tittery little exclamations of rage. "Go away. You're mad. I shall call the police."

Celia put a photograph on his desk. "If you do, I shall send that to the *Haxton Gazette*."

Timothy looked at the photo in dismay, then pushed it aside, and composed his chins pompously. "Do if you like, I have nothing to hide. My relationship with Hodson is a purely business one, concerning the land he wants to buy."

"But Hodson's office is in the sales shed," Celia objected.

"Yes," added Bill very softly. "What were you doing going into the Old Manor House, eh? You were after the girlies, weren't you, you horny senile lecher you. Thought no one saw you creeping into the cat house, did you? I'm ashamed of you."

As Celia had foreseen, Bill was a smash hit in the role of clean puritanical youth rebuking the unattractive lusts of middle age. The effect on Timothy was magical. Panic-stricken little moans escaped from him. He was bright red.

"If you don't want a scandal," said Celia, "you'd better tell me what's happened to Deirdre."

Timothy began moaning a little louder, like a kettle coming to the boil. "You're mad," he managed. "The whole village knows you're mad."

Bill made a fierce, quickly checked movement.

"No Bill, you're not to hit him," said Celia sharply. "Timothy, please be careful, he has a hot temper when provoked."

"No more nasty talk like that, you hear?" Bill added.

"Let me make it easy for you," said Celia. "Here's a multiple-

126

choice question, delete words not applicable. Your wife is missing because *a*, you have murdered her, *b*, she has been abducted and murdered by persons unknown, or *c*, disgusted by your whoremongering she has gone off with someone else."

"I'm not talking to you about this, Celia."

"Why not?"

"Deirdre says I'm not to tell anyone where she is," Timothy blurted out in what was obviously a moment of truth.

So Deirdre was alive, which eliminated *a* and *b*. A lover, then? One with enough influence on her to make her remove herself conveniently when Celia made her discovery at The Towers? If so, there were only two possibilities.

"Which of them is it, Timothy? Nigel or Roy?"

"Go away, Celia, I'm not telling you anything."

She produced a further selection of the photographs she had taken from the tree, and spread them out on the desk. "D'you want me to send a set of these to every women's organisation in Haxton? Town councillors, local worthies, the lot, all trooping into the Old Manor House like mice after the cheese?"

"Oh Celia," Timothy pleaded, "why are you stirring up all this trouble?"

"To keep my pet rabbit amused, so that it doesn't run away to sea. Come on, you'll have to start talking sooner or later. Who is it?"

"If I tell you a bit about this," said Timothy, sweating heavily, "will you swear not to pass it on to Nigel Fitzgerald?"

Celia gaped. This was fascinating. "Did Deirdre say it was important for Nigel not to know?"

"Actually, yes."

Then Nigel was not the lover, obviously. "How long has her thing with Roy Armitage been going on?" she demanded.

"I didn't say Roy . . ."

"Stop fussing, and answer my question."

"I . . . don't remember."

"Yes you do, make an effort. When did you and Deirdre start having rows because your evening meal was always late?"

"Some time in the autumn, I think. And then . . ."

"Yes. Go on."

"One night just before Christmas she wasn't home till after nine and I asked her where the hell she'd been and she came right out with it, she'd been with Roy."

"I see, and in view of your lunch hour activities she thought that perfectly fair. Where did they meet?"

"It's none of your business. Anyway I don't know."

He did know, but how could he be made to tell? She was about to brandish the incriminating photos again when light dawned. Something Alison had told her in the autumn fitted suddenly into place, she could answer the question herself. "They met at The Towers, didn't they, Timothy?"

"Yes, damn you, but what business is all this of yours? I shall get one of the partners to help me throw you out."

"Don't get naughty, Mr Foster," Bill snapped. "We're not having that sort of talk."

"Now, Timothy," Celia went on, "was Deirdre with Roy on the evening when the Emersons were murdered?"

"I . . . don't know."

"Nonsense, of course you do. The police spent the whole weekend knocking on doors and asking people where they'd been that night and whether they'd seen or heard anything. What did Deirdre say when they asked her?"

"She . . . said she was at home."

"And was that true?"

"No, blast you."

"She was with Roy, but didn't want to admit it to the police, so she lied and made you back her up, right?"

"Why not? Her being with Roy wasn't relevant, she had nothing to do with the Emersons being killed."

Celia had been thinking fast and alarm bells were ringing in her mind. "Timothy, you are going to tell me where Deirdre is."

"No, I've talked too much already."

"Don't argue. She's in very great danger. She was with Roy at The Towers on the evening when the Emersons were killed, I think she knows something that Roy doesn't want her to tell me, something that would make sense to me though it doesn't to her. D'you want Bill to start knocking your teeth out or will you give me her address and phone number?"

"I can't. I've talked too much already."

"Why not? Can't you grasp that she's in danger?"

"I daren't, she's blackmailing me, like you are, about me going to . . . the Hodson place. The senior partners here don't like me. I've made some mistakes, they're looking for an excuse to throw me out, and she says she'll make a huge scandal if I tell anyone where she is or make a fuss about her and Roy."

"I tell you what we do then," Bill suggested. "Fair's fair, you tell us her address, we tell her we got it off one of them spy satellites, Deirdre doesn't tell your boss about you and the cat house, and I don't knock your teeth out, okay?"

After a little more argument he caved in. Deirdre, he said, had got herself a job as receptionist at the Grosvenor Hotel in Southcliff-on-Sea.

"And I think he was telling the truth," said Celia as they sped towards the coast. "Deirdre would have to have a job, Roy's far too hard up to keep her in idleness."

They were travelling in Celia's pick-up—the motorcycle was too vulnerable. A sudden lane change by a car they were overtaking, a skid, it was too easy to arrange.

"You told me Deirdre's nice looking," said Bill. "What would she want with a funny little ferret like Roy?"

"Ferrets fascinate some women, I gather. My husband was in the army for a bit; according to him the ferrety little men in the battalion could be in bed and out again twice while the gorgeous six-footers were still floundering and groping at first base."

He gave a hoot of laughter. "D'you think I floundered and groped when I met that girl in London and decided it was serious?"

"Oh Bill, I do apologise. I wasn't thinking."

"Your old man missed the point. If you're a funny little ferret you need to keep proving things to yourself that others don't. One thing puzzles me though. How did you work out that Deirdre and Roy went to The Towers to do it?"

"Ah, I remembered something that happened back in the autumn. Alison had rather bad flu, and Roy suddenly said he'd sleep in the house till she was better, which was a dramatic change of attitude. Up to then he hadn't so much as changed a light bulb for her, so why would he suddenly risk catching flu? He'd got Boxie to put his old childhood bedroom in order so that he could sleep there whenever there was a crisis, and it's up on the second floor out of the way, and it suddenly made sense."

"Funny place to choose, though," said Bill. "You'd think there was enough going on at The Towers without them two popping in for a bit of healthy exercise. There's Nellie doing her forging and Alison having hysterics and that Boxie locking and unlocking everything, how could they concentrate?"

"Nobody uses the second floor, you see, and I expect he's arranged things so that Boxie doesn't have to let them in, some way of smuggling her through the security barrier and up the back stairs. Another thing, the timing's always puzzled me. Deirdre stopped work at four, I never kept her later if I could help it, she had plenty of time to fornicate and then cook. So why was Timothy's evening meal always late? Don't you see, they had to wait till Nigel had gone off to the pub to eat, otherwise he'd have realised what was going on. And for some reason Nigel mustn't know."

The flat landscape had taken on the windswept, unfinished look of areas just behind the coast. Soon they were in the outskirts of Southcliff. It was a small, exclusive resort consisting of a golf course, some large, well-kept holiday houses and the Grosvenor Hotel, facing across carefully tended lawns towards a pebble beach. It was early in the season and in the dead hours of a weekday afternoon its entrance hall was deserted except for Deirdre Foster, who sat knitting behind the reception desk.

"Hullo, Deirdre," said Celia.

Deirdre went on knitting for almost a minute. "I don't want to talk to you. How did you find out I was here?"

"Detective agency," Celia lied. "We must talk, you probably don't realise that you're in danger."

Deirdre ignored this and went on knitting.

"Oh do stop fiddling with that hellish wool and pay attention. It's not safe for you to stay here under Roy's thumb."

"You're mad, you stir up trouble and accuse people of stealing things when they haven't."

"That was a trap set for me to fall into, so that no one would believe me about the body in the flowerbed. You're in danger, really you are. You know too much."

"There's nothing for me to know too much about."

"Think, Deirdre. There's something you know without realising it's important, something that happened at The Towers that night when the Emersons were killed. You were there, weren't you?"

She put down her knitting for emphasis. "Yes. I was, and nothing happened there. No one buried a corpse in the garden for you to find in one of your crazy fits, no one even knew the Emersons were being killed on the other side of Butler's Copse. Can't you get it into your head? *No* corpse, *no* burying anything in a flowerbed, not even a three-act screaming fit from Alison because she'd seen a mouse in the pantry. Nothing, nothing, nothing. I know nothing happened, because I was there."

"Upstairs with Roy."

"Yes. Why not?"

"No reason at all as far as I'm concerned. But if you're lying to shield Roy . . ."

"I am not lying to shield Roy," said Deirdre in a voice strangled with fury. She ducked down and searched for something in the shelves under the reception desk. "Perhaps this will shut you up."

She surfaced again with a copy of the *Haxton Gazette*, folded with an inner page uppermost and slapped it down in front of Celia. "If that won't stop your nonsense I don't know what will."

Celia read the short item. Kenny Cooper, who disappeared from his home in Westfield immediately after the Emersons' murder, had been arrested for shoplifting in Brighton.

TWELVE

THEY STARTED BACK to Archerscroft in silence. The embarrassment-sulk was firmly installed on Bill's face. Celia stared ahead at
the road, too numb to think.

"D'you want to move out and go back to Haxton?" she asked
abruptly. "I shan't blame you if you do."

There was a long silence. "No, Celia."

"But you must be saying to yourself, 'she raised a false scare
about a corpse that wasn't there and she couldn't face the fact that
she'd made an utter fool of herself, so she dreamed up this huge
conspiracy to prove to herself that she was right and everyone else
was wrong.'"

"Yes," said Bill. "I thought about that. Then I remembered the
wine bottle in the potting shed."

"I could have rigged that up before we left for Melsingham, just
to fool you."

"That's right, you could have. But it was taken away again after
we'd gone back into the house, how did you fix that then? You
never dreamed up no conspiracy, Celia, but we have to look at it
different now."

"This has knocked me bottom side up, I can't look at it at all."

But after a few more miles her brain suddenly started to work
again. "Bill, did anything about that conversation strike you as
odd?"

"I dunno. What specially?"

"Looking back, it seems a strange way for her to behave. She
could have shut me up in ten seconds by saying, 'Kenny Cooper's
alive and here's the newspaper to prove it.' She didn't, she went on

132

and on about no corpse, nothing buried in the garden, not even a minor emergency to make Alison scream. Why? Because Kenny not being dead wasn't the point. The message she had to get across was that *nobody* was killed that night at The Towers."

"Oh Celia! You have something there. Kenny's still walking around, so . . ."

"It wasn't his foot I saw, and we have to decide whose it was."

"That's right, we put out the dragnet like for Cinderella."

"Except that there's an obvious favourite for the Cinderella stakes."

"That's right! Nigel and Roy went and nobbled Cinderella in the stables, for fear he'd make trouble with Nellie over them pictures."

"I still think that's overkill," Celia objected. "Would they slaughter poor Mr Peeters just to cover up a forgery?"

"Those two might, they're crazy as pavements."

"And how do the Emersons fit in?"

"I dunno, but we have to find out if this Peeters is still in his stable eating his hay. D'you have his phone number?"

"Yes. In my bag."

Back at Archerscroft she hurried into the house, trying to think of a tactful way of asking a Dutch art dealer whether or not he was dead. As she picked up the phone there was a slight noise behind her. She turned. Nigel Fitzgerald stood blocking her way of escape. In her excitement she had forgotten to let Bill go in first.

"Hullo Celia," said Nigel, with a smile that was also a threat. "I was worried about you so I came. You've heard the news?"

"What news?"

"Kenny Cooper's turned up. The police arrested him in Brighton."

"Yes, I had heard," said Celia, thinking hard. At any moment Bill would join them and the situation would be easier to handle.

"I don't know what to say to you, except that I'm sorry. It must have been an appalling shock to you."

But out in the yard Bill's motorcycle burst into a roar and shot away. She listened, bewildered and terrified, while its exhaust note faded away down the lane.

"Well, his departure was to be expected," said Nigel. "It must have been a shock to him too, finding out that this whole great conspiracy of yours existed only in your imagination. But I do think he could have waited to say goodbye."

They were standing in her tiny office, close together. She needed room for manoeuvre as well as time to think.

"D'you mind if I sit down?" she asked, and moved towards the living room.

He stepped aside, but kept close to her and posted himself in front of her chair when she sat down.

"Poor Celia," he went on. "You'll have to clear out of Westfield, of course, you've made too many enemies here, and you'll never live the Kenny Cooper thing down. I suppose you could start again somewhere else, but seriously my dear, is it worth the effort? You have this difficult temperament, you'll make the same mistakes again and again . . ."

He was wearing gloves. There was something clutched in his left hand, something small like a bottle of pills. His intention was abominably clear.

"But in the last analysis, Celia, it's not what others think of you, one can ignore them, it's whether you can live with yourself when you've reached the bottom of the pit. And being an ageing lesbian doesn't help."

An ageing lesbian. *So he believed that.*

He must believe it, otherwise there was no point in saying it. The implications took a moment to sink in. When they did she knew there was hope, saw at once what her line of attack should be.

"Who told you?" she asked.

"It's all over the village, I'm afraid, after the business with Deirdre."

"But who told you that Deirdre had fled from my disgusting embraces?"

"I don't remember. Is it important?"

"Yes. Think. Someone in your family?"

134

"Oh. Yes, it was my Uncle Roy."

"I thought as much. He had to fudge up some story. Otherwise you'd have wondered why Deirdre agreed to make herself scarce exactly at the right moment, so I wouldn't have a witness when he started trying to prove that I was mad."

"You're denying that you made a pass at Deirdre?"

"Of course. Why is Roy keeping the truth from you? Why aren't you allowed to know that he and Deirdre are lovers?"

After thinking about this, he said, "They aren't, you're making this up."

"Timothy says they are. He's her husband, surely he would know? He also says you mustn't be told on pain of Deirdre's severe displeasure."

"If you're not lying Timothy is," he said.

"Deirdre herself admits it."

"How d'you know?"

"I've talked to her, she's working as a receptionist at the Grosvenor Hotel in Southcliff-on-Sea. Ring them and check if you don't believe me."

But the phone was in her office. She watched him decide not to make the call. Apart from leaving her to her own devices it would mean admitting that he was beginning to have his doubts.

"You're lying," he repeated. But it sounded more like a question.

"Well, you must make up your own mind about that, but do go on with what you were saying. I think you were trying to talk me into taking an overdose."

"My God Celia, you're tough, aren't you, under all that fragile prettiness and silver hair."

"Yes, but it's time you leant over me and said, 'do you ever have a death wish?' in a thrilling sort of voice."

Nigel frowned. "I told Uncle Roy it wouldn't work."

"No it won't, and nor will Plan B, which I suppose is to fix up something that will look like suicide." With a sudden movement she swept everything off the sideboard behind her, littering the floor with fragments of crockery and with the contents of a

135

smashed sherry bottle. "That's what they call 'signs of a struggle' at inquests, and the real struggle will start the moment you lay a finger on me, I shall bite and kick and scratch and make sure I end up as a very damaged corpse. No way will you be able to make me look like a suicide, so you'd better have a rethink."

He stood there, tossing the bottle of pills lightly from one hand to the other. "He couldn't be having an affair with Deirdre. Harriet's found out that he's as randy as a buck-rabbit, she makes him account for every minute of his day."

"Except when he goes to The Towers to give your mother moral support, that's allowed, isn't it?"

"Yes. Well?"

"The moral support for your mother increased sharply last autumn, coinciding with a marked improvement in the bedroom arrangements on the second floor. And that in turn coincided with the start of his thing with Deirdre."

He laughed, but without conviction. "Come off it, Celia. If they were meeting at The Towers I'd have seen them come and go."

"No, because that happened while you were eating at the pub. Did he have a way of getting in and out without going through all that palaver with Boxie?"

"Yes, he's put one of the circuits on the burglar alarm out of action. He said if Alison thought it was working okay she'd feel safe and that was all that mattered."

"Which circuit?"

"The one guarding the door to the yard at the bottom of the back stairs."

"And what excuse did he give for needing to get into the house without Alison knowing?"

"It wasn't an excuse, there's some marvellous wine in the cellar that my grandfather laid down, the port's fantastic. He helps himself to the odd bottle from time to time and gives me some. Alison would be furious, she thinks it's going to be sold for millions when it's matured a bit more."

"And that was his excuse for sabotaging the burglar alarm? And you believed it? My poor Nigel, a babe in arms could march out of

136

the front door under Boxie's nose with a bottle of port hidden under its overcoat."

"Oh . . ."

"If they could come and go by that door near the bottom of the back stairs, he could get her up to his love-nest on the second floor and no one any the wiser."

He looked at her with infinitely sad eyes. She knew now that she was winning.

"Concentrate, Nigel. Use your brains. He's lied to you, he's used you, what's the next trick he's going to play on you? Why mustn't you know about him and Deirdre?"

"Because . . ." Suddenly he was staring into space as if he had been hit on the head. "My God, how could I have been so dim!" He threw the bottle of pills into the fireplace. "Celia, I'm going to get you out of this mess."

"You're changing sides?"

"Yes. Quick, we must find Wilkins before Roy gets back."

"He's still here?"

"Yes, he'll be somewhere in the outbuildings, it was my ingenious uncle who went off on the motorcycle, after bashing Wilkins on the head with something heavy."

They found Bill lying on the floor of the potting shed with his hands and feet tied. He was moaning and bleeding heavily from a scalp wound.

"Hospital," said Nigel.

"I'll ring for an ambulance."

"No, Uncle Roy will be back any moment to collect him and reunite him with his bike. The idea is an artistically managed road accident, as if he'd taken a bend too fast. We must get him into your pick-up. What can we use as a stretcher?"

"A hurdle. There are some in the pile beside the compost heap."

He fetched one, and they eased Bill gently into the back of the pick-up. "Will you drive?" she asked.

He thought for a moment before answering. "No, there are things I have to attend to. Take him to Casualty at Haxton Hospital and stay there with him, that's very important, don't move out of the hospital on any account. Wait there till I call for you, then I'll know you're safe."

"Very well. Why have you changed sides, Nigel?"

He wondered about this. "I don't think I have. I've always been on my mother's side and nobody else's and I still am."

"He's severely concussed, Mrs Grant," said the charge sister, "and we shan't know any more till the X-rays have been looked at. Why don't you go home and rest and ring us in about three hours' time?"

"No," said Celia. "There's someone coming here to meet me, I can't leave. But, oh dear, I have some expensive international calls to make, where can I make them without putting coins in the slot every other second?"

This was something, it seemed, that the relatives of accident patients often asked for. The charge nurse told her what the arrangements were and left her to it.

The Amsterdam number answered almost at once. "May I speak to Dr Jan Peeters, please? . . . Yes, I suppose it is a business matter really. I understand he was in England some months ago investigating an art forgery, and I'd like to get in touch with him. . . . Oh? You mean, he's still here? Oh! Oh my dear Mrs Peeters, I am sorry, how very distressing for you. When did this happen, I mean when was he last seen? . . . I see. Yes of course I will, who is in charge of the investigation? Inspector Barrington at New Scotland Yard. . . . Yes, I'll ring him first thing tomorrow in case there's any relevant information I can give. . . . No, Mrs Peeters, I didn't meet your husband, but I think his enquiries overlapped with some of mine. Yes. Oh, I do understand, I hope they manage to trace him."

What a hypocrite I am, she thought guiltily. The last time Peeters was seen alive was on the morning of the Emerson murder. While she condoled with Mrs Peeters, she had been thinking, "Hurrah, I've got a body to attach to that foot."

Her next call was to the Philadelphia Museum of Art, where her enquiry was transferred from extension to extension: Had they

138

had a recent request for a reproduction of their Van den Berghe flower-piece?

"I'm enquiring into a forgery," she explained, "done by someone who must have had a copy of your picture in front of them. There is?* How big is it? . . . No, I don't think so, a forger would want something bigger to work from and in colour. Ah, that sounds more like it, who asked for it? . . . And the address? Thank you so much. Now I have one more question if you can bear it. Did you have any correspondence about your Van den Berghe with a Dr Jan Peeters of Amsterdam? I think he may have been on the same track as myself, asking if anyone had asked for a reproduction, and if so who . . . Yes, I realise that you would normally treat another scholar's enquiries as confidential, but Dr Peeters is listed as a missing person, we're all very afraid that something must have happened to him, so please don't be difficult. . . . He did. Oh, thank you, that's very helpful. And the date of your letter? Thank you, I'm sorry to have put you to so much trouble."

Here was another loose end satisfactorily tidied up. But how badly was Bill hurt? Surely there must be news by now?

"There's no fracture," said the house surgeon, brandishing an X-ray of Bill's skull. "Only severe concussion and a nasty scalp wound."

"Oh, what a relief. Can I see him?"

"Well . . . are you a relative?"

"No, only his employer."

"Then I think perhaps not. Tomorrow or the next day."

Outside it was getting dark. Two hours had passed since she arrived at the hospital, how much longer would she have to wait around for Nigel? Very soon the nurses would be staring at her and wondering why she did not go home.

She rang Nigel's number in the flat at The Towers. No reply, so she rang Archerscroft on the offchance. A man's voice answered. "Mrs Grant?"

*There is a reproduction of the Philadelphia picture in Mitchell, *European Flower Painters* (Schiedam, 1981) but it is in black and white and very small.

139

"Yes. Who is that?"

"Inspector Rawlings, Haxton CID. We've been trying to contact you. Could you come back here as soon as possible, please?"

"Why? What's happened?"

"I'd prefer you to come here and let me explain. Where are you speaking from?"

"Haxton Hospital." She thought for a moment. "I'll come if you send a car for me."

"Why? Have you no transport?"

"Yes, but I have survived two attempts to murder me in the last twenty-four hours, I'd feel safer in a police car."

The car came, but the driver either did not know or had been told not to say what was wrong at Archerscroft. She arrived there to find police cars flashing their blue lights idiotically, to make sure that everyone for miles around knew that poor mad Mrs Grant was in trouble again. She jumped out and made for the back door, but a tall policeman headed her off.

"Mrs Grant? I'm Inspector Rawlings, I'd rather you came in the front way."

"Oh, why? Please tell me what has happened."

"A man has been killed. He was found by a lady delivering the parish magazine, lying outside your back door."

"Oh no! Which of them is it, Roy or Nigel?"

"It's a Mr Armitage, is his name Roy? How did you know, Mrs Grant, that it would be one of those two?"

"Now, Mrs Grant," said Rawlings. "Let's hear your explanation."

He had taken her into the living room. Sergeant Parsons was there with his notebook and pencil poised, and determination to disbelieve written all over his bearded face.

"I'm afraid this will take some time," said Celia. "But shall we start with the unfortunate Dr Jan Peeters, who came to England two months ago to investigate a series of art forgeries, on which he is an expert. His wife says he's been missing since the day of the Emerson murder, when he checked out of his London hotel and

140

drove away in a self-drive hire car which has since been found abandoned in central London. Sergeant Parsons, you'll never remember all this, aren't you going to take any of it down?"

Parsons shrugged, and made contemptuous passes in his notebook with the pencil.

"Here's Dr Peeters' address and phone number in Amsterdam. His disappearance is being investigated by Inspector Barrington of the forgeries squad at Scotland Yard. The next bit's complicated. I don't want to bore you with a lecture on the history of art, but the essential point is that Peeters' enquiries led him to 15, East Street in Haxton, the home of an elderly couple called Wilson. They will recognise a photograph of Dr Peeters if shown one, and will tell you that he called there to ask about a large envelope which arrived there from the Philadelphia Museum of Art. However, it was not addressed to them but to Mrs Wilson's sister, a Mrs Box. They were being used as an accommodation address."

"All this is very interesting, Mrs Grant," said Inspector Rawlings. "But how does it relate to the death of Mr Armitage?"

"Mrs Box is Lady Armitage's cook, and Lady Armitage is Mr Armitage's mother. On discovering where Mrs Box was employed, and knowing what the envelope from Philadelphia contained, he deduced that the forger was to be found at The Towers, and was confirmed in his suspicion when he learnt that Lady Armitage was an accomplished flower painter. He therefore went to The Towers, and I need hardly add that the foot I unearthed in Lady Armitage's herbaceous border belonged to him and not to Kenny Cooper."

Sergeant Parsons hissed impatiently into his beard. "I examined the flowerbed, Inspector, and satisfied myself that there was no body in it."

"By then it had been taken away, we've had this argument before."

They both looked at Inspector Rawlings and waited.

"You've made some very serious accusations, Mrs Grant. We'll check with Inspector Barrington at the Yard, but there's a lot that depends on your word alone, and . . ."

"I know, it will all look very different when you've found Dr Peeters' body."

"But we have no idea where to look for it."

"Oh, but I have," said Celia.

THIRTEEN

CELIA STUDIED INSPECTOR Barrington of the forgeries squad as he sat opposite her in what had once been Roger's favourite armchair. He was a good looking fifty-year-old with curly grey hair trendily cut, more like an actor than a policeman, and his warm praise of her detective powers were delivered with actorish charm. He seemed to have taken over the whole conduct of the case from Rawlings and Parsons.

"I must be sure of my ground, Mrs Grant, a mistake would be very embarrassing. Suppose Dr Peeters' remains aren't where you suspect?"

"You'll have to take a snap decision when you get there. Surely it's possible to tell whether flagstones have recently been taken up?"

"In the kitchen premises, you say. Where, exactly?"

"I don't know, that sort of house has acres of stone-flagged sculleries and pantries and larders, you'll have to look for a place where the paving has been disturbed."

"You've been brilliantly right so far, Mrs Grant, but how can you be so sure I'll find one?"

"I told you, the cinerarias had gone from the front hall. Why? The display was good for another fortnight at least. She had to get rid of them because she wanted to put in a mass of heliotrope and stephanotis instead, the most heavily scented things that are in flower at this time of year. And why were there onions boiling on the stove at four in the afternoon? Surely it's obvious."

Inspector Barrington patted his handsome curls. "You're surely not suggesting that the decomposing remains were brought into

143

the house and kept there while a hole was dug under the floor to accommodate them? And that a few onions and pot plants were enough to mask the smell? With all respect, Mrs Grant . . ."

"Oh no, the house would have been quite uninhabitable, the stench while I was digging was quite nauseating. When you go there you'll see that the tower has a sort of gazebo on top of it, open to the winds on all four sides. I think they put him up there till the hole was ready, it's too high for him to be smelt at ground level, though I did imagine I caught a whiff one day when I was working in the garden. The panic I described to you, when I wasn't allowed in the kitchen, was because I'd arrived during or just after the, shall we say, most delicate phase of the operation."

Barrington thought for a moment, then rose. "Very well, I shall go there and see what I find."

"Oh, please don't go yet, I've a lot more to tell you. For instance, a letter arrived this morning that I think you ought to see. It's from Nigel Fitzgerald."

He took the letter from its envelope, then looked at the postmark. "London Airport, yesterday afternoon," he murmured, and began to read.

Dear Celia,

I'm afraid I never intended to keep my date with you at the hospital. It has been clear for some time that I would have to seek my fortune abroad, and by the time you get this I shall have started to do so. My Uncle Roy and I procured false passports for use in emergency some time ago.

I'm sorry I gave you such a rough time. It looked at first as if this whole thing could be swept under the carpet, so I went along with Uncle Roy and did my best to help. I changed sides partly because you had obviously found out far too much; and partly for a reason which I will explain in a moment.

You have displayed a robust commonsense throughout this affair, and you also have a social conscience. That is why I am writing to you. Unavoidably I have left chaos behind me at The Towers, and neither my mother nor my grandmother is capable of taking sensible decisions. I want you, please, to go up there as soon as possible and take charge.

My mother must be got into a psychiatric hospital at once. She is in a frightful state and will probably have to live permanently in an institution. This means that my grandmother must be moved into a home of some kind, no paid companion would tolerate conditions at The Towers. Boxie can go to her sister and brother-in-law in Haxton.

You will be wondering about money. My grandmother is living on an annuity which dies with her. Under my grandfather's will The Towers and his botanical library and herbarium go on her death to the Royal Horticultural Society to be turned into a museum, a prospect which horrifies them. These arrangements leave my mother with no home, no income and no house to sell. I think you know how the family set out to solve this problem.

I'm still wondering why I let myself be conned by Uncle Roy for so long. He's quite a formidable person, rather frightening really, in fact I now realise that he is more than half-mad, but I've always admired the ruthless way he arranges everything for his own satisfaction, and of course I was grateful for what he was doing about my mother's finances. The whole scheme was his idea.

We managed to build up quite an impressive sum for her, but she has always been incapable of looking after money, so it seemed quite natural that Uncle Roy should act as treasurer. After a time I discovered quite by accident that some of the investments were in his name and not in my mother's. He said he'd arranged it that way to save her trouble but it worried me a little. Not about embezzlement, that hadn't occurred to me. I simply said wasn't that a bit unwise, suppose something happened to him?

He was very nice about it and said of course he saw my point. To meet it he made a will with my mother as sole beneficiary, it's lodged with the family solicitors. I didn't spot the reasons for his rather odd financial arrangements till yesterday, when it hit me like a thunderbolt. He's a very sexy man, he's had several passionate affairs with women. He loathes Aunt Harriet, but she's his meal ticket and he's always managed to talk her out of divorcing him. So far, that is. But when you told me about him and Deirdre the penny suddenly dropped. He's never intended the money for my mother, he'd dreamed up the whole scheme to finance a rosy future somewhere abroad for him and Deirdre. He was afraid I'd rumble him if I knew he was in love with Deirdre, that was why I mustn't be told.

I'm sorry to leave you with such an untidy mess to clear up. As I told you, I have always been on my mother's side and no one else's, and I've done my best for her. Uncle Roy's executors may have trouble getting odd sums back from numbered accounts in Switzerland and so on, but there should be enough to keep her in reasonable comfort for the rest of her life.

Yours, with thanks in anticipation,

Nigel Fitzgerald.

"So there you have Roy Armitage's motive for killing Dr Peeters," said Celia, as Barrington put the letter back in its envelope. "And Nigel's for killing Roy."

Barrington's eyes met hers. "Yes. Yes."

"There's one more thing. I'm worried about Kenny Cooper. He's not very bright and if the Haxton CID press him hard enough he'll probably confess to a crime he didn't commit. It's so embarrassing for the police when people retract their confession afterwards and say it was given under duress."

"Kenny Cooper? Oh yes, the boy they're holding for the murder of Mr and Mrs Emerson. It sounded to me as if he was guilty."

"I don't think so, let me explain . . ."

She had already argued this out with the Haxton police. Kenny's story was that he was cutting through Butler's Copse for an appointment with Nigel Fitzgerald, in connection with a joke notice to be put up in huge letters outside the village church. On his way he passed near the end of the Emersons' garden and saw them lying in the shaft of light from their open back door, and had gone closer to investigate. When he saw what had happened he had been moved by normal human compassion and had knelt down beside them to give assistance, then realised that they were dead and that he was the last person who should be found beside two dead bodies at Wheelwright's Cottage, which he was known to have broken into on several previous occasions. There was blood on his clothes, for all he knew he had left fingerprints and he had been blamed before for crimes he did not commit. So he panicked and ran.

Rawlings had given him a rough time, especially over his unlikely sounding claim to have an appointment that night with Nigel Fitzgerald, who was not available to confirm it.

"But he did help Nigel with his practical jokes," Celia told Barrington. "He may well have been on his way there that night."

"Oh, I daren't interfere, Mrs Grant. Haxton CID are furious with me for taking the Armitage case away from them, I can't muscle in on another case of theirs."

"But surely the two could be connected? Wheelwright's Cottage is within a few hundred yards of The Towers. There was a trail of blood leading away from Wheelwright's into the wood, the theory was that the Emersons had wounded their attacker. Inspector Rawlings was going to check the blood group against Kenny's, surely you're entitled to know the result?"

"Yes. Yes, I think you're right. May I use your phone?"

While he was phoning Celia wondered why she had taken an instant dislike to him. He was pleasant-looking and intelligent and had grasped very quickly that far from being a semi-lunatic busybody she was talking perfect sense. Nevertheless . . .

He came back from the telephone. "Young Cooper is blood group A. The trail through the wood was O rhesus negative. It must have come from an accomplice, they're going to question him again."

"Oh what nonsense, the trail wasn't anybody running into the wood, it was Dr Peeters going the opposite way. It's clear what happened. Dr Peeters was one of those ox-like six-foot Dutchmen and Roy Armitage, who is tiny, made a mess of it and didn't kill him outright. Peeters got away from him into the wood and stumbled towards a light he saw on the far side, hoping to find help. By the time Roy Armitage caught up with him he was explaining to the Emersons with his dying breath how he came to have knife or bullet wounds or whatever. So when Roy had finished him off, he had to go to work on the Emersons with that axe."

There was a long silence. They looked at each other like conspirators, afraid to put their thoughts into words.

"Yes," said Barrington. "Yes, that's a credible explanation of what happened. Fortunately Roy Armitage is dead, defending counsel would make mincemeat of it if it came to trial."

FOURTEEN

CLAD IN THE deepest mourning, Harriet Armitage sat in the front pew of the crematorium chapel, overacting grotesquely her role as the sorrowing widow of a man she could not conceivably regret. Deirdre Foster had abandoned her declared intention of draping herself from head to foot in black and occupying the other front pew in a bid for co-widow status. A commonsensical lecture from Celia, plus the fact that Roy's will left her nothing, had persuaded her that it would be wiser to don less eyecatching garb and sit sobbing gently beside her Timothy a few rows back.

Alison was not in the congregation, being under heavy sedation in a psychiatric hospital. But Nellie, grim-faced but dry-eyed, had made a state entry in a wheelchair pushed by Celia. Many local People Like Us had thought it proper to put in an appearance and villagers agog with curiosity filled the back pews.

Roy Armitage lay coffined before them. The verdict at the inquest had been murder by a person or persons unknown, with a rider from the jury suggesting hopefully that Nigel Fitzgerald should be traced and questioned. Rumours were flying round the village, all discreditable to Celia. It was typical of her, everyone felt, to have dead gentlemen lying in her back yard.

The doors of the furnace slid open and Roy rolled slowly into it. With the mourners for the next funeral pressing on their heels, the congregation was ushered out through a side door into the Garden of Rest, where the wreaths were laid out for inspection.

"Well Harriet?" Nellie called from her wheelchair. "What do you plan to do now?"

"I shall travel for a time, to get over the shock," said Harriet, in the voice she used for Lady Bracknell with the Village Players.

"Running away, are you, in case I try to billet myself on you? I might, The Towers is uninhabitable without Alison."

"There's no question of that, we're not blood relations," snapped Harriet.

"Don't worry, dear, I was only joking. Celia's found me a private hotel full of old tabby cats, I shall move in there and bully them all."

Nellie had put on a brave show and had spent her time countering Barrington's enquiries with outrageous lies. According to her she had acted in innocent good faith when producing flower-pieces in the Dutch style for people who could not afford the real thing. She had no idea that Mrs Slansky, who had vanished without trace from her gallery in London, was passing them off as genuine. As for the hole in the scullery floor and its gruesome contents, she had asked Nigel and Roy what was going on and had been told that the drains were being dealt with and they should keep away because of the unpleasant smell. Barrington did not believe a word of her nonsense, but in the absence of Nigel, Roy and Mrs Slansky he was finding it difficult to disprove.

As Celia pushed Nellie's wheelchair along the row of wreaths Ethel Cooper came past.

"So you got your Kenny back safe and sound," said Celia. "I'm so glad."

"No thanks to you," said Ethel and moved on. Two villagers who had heard the exchange nodded approval and looked daggers at Celia.

That finally decided it. Westfield was a snake pit, she was going to sell Archerscroft and get out.

Next day she went to the hospital to break the news of this decision to Bill. He was sitting up by his bedside, but his hair was a sight, with the brown dye growing out of the bits which had not been shaved off to treat the scalp wound.

"I've screwed Hodson up to sixty-five thousand," she told him, "which means that I can afford to offer you a decent salary when I start up elsewhere. That is, if you want to come."

150

"Oh Celia, yes please. I like working with you. The more I think the more I see how clever you are. I see now that the cleverest thing of all is how you've tidied everything up nice at The Towers after the mess they all made there."

He was looking at her oddly.

"Bill, I'm not sure I understand what you mean."

"Oh Celia. You do."

"Oh. Bother. I didn't think you'd spot it."

"I only spotted it because I remembered what you said about overkill."

"You won't tell anyone, will you?"

"So long as you don't dig up no more Dutchmen with their guts all slit to ribbons with carving knives."

Dr Peeters' remains had been exhumed from under the scullery floor at The Towers. He had died, it seemed, from stomach wounds inflicted by something like a kitchen knife. The date of the inquest had been fixed and Celia had asked Inspector Barrington whether her evidence should include a full account of her discoveries concerning the fake Van den Berghe.

"I've been wondering, Mrs Grant, whether you'll need to give evidence at all. I could include the point about the Philadelphia Museum and so on in my evidence. It's always a mistake to confuse an inquest jury with too much detail."

She had been right, he was like an actor, the sort who steals the best lines from the rest of the case. He would probably be too busy hogging the limelight to mention that Peeters had originally gone to his rest under a herbaceous border, and that but for poor mad Mrs Grant who always got everything wrong, he would still be there.

"If you leave it to me," Barrington told her, "I think I can get the jury to bring in a verdict of murder against Mr Armitage, which would be the most satisfactory result for all concerned."

He is blackmailing me, Celia thought, and I have to submit to blackmail. If I let him hog the limelight at the inquest he will not mention the secret we share, though neither of us has put it into words.

Murdering Jan Peeters was an absurd piece of overkill. Forging a picture was not a very awful crime. Roy and Nellie between them could have talked their way out of serious trouble, as Nellie was doing now, by throwing all the blame on Mrs Slansky. If Roy had been forced to kill as a last resort, he would not have made a mess of it and let Peeters get away through the wood and raise the alarm.

But poor, crazed Alison was a different matter. One could imagine her panic, suddenly confronted with a man who put terrifying questions, threatened exposure, prosecution, perhaps confiscation of the nest egg she relied on to live after Nellie died. One could imagine her fetching a kitchen knife, stabbing savagely but not savagely enough, then screaming and screaming till Roy came pounding downstairs pulling on his clothes and dashing out into the night in search of Peeters.

Roy had killed the Emersons and hidden Peeters' corpse to protect Alison. With her in jail he would be saddled with looking after his mother, and if Peeters was found and identified the forgeries would be traced to Nellie. Among other disagreeable consequences of that, the nest egg he had earmarked for himself and Deirdre would be in danger.

When Nigel came back from his dinner at the pub, Roy had told him what had happened. Nigel agreed at once to help cover up the crime, to protect his mother.

Barrington knew that Alison had killed Peeters, but he had said nothing. It was impossible to prove, Alison could never have been brought to trial even if she was fit to plead. But a cruel word from him at the inquest would have crushed her under a mountain of gossiping suspicion from which no psychiatrist could rescue her, and he would utter it unless Celia let him have his way.

So she decided to let him hog the limelight and play down the key part she had played in the whole affair. The village would go on thinking of her as poor mad Mrs Grant, but that hardly mattered. She would remove herself and her primroses elsewhere.

They were looking good. They might not come true from seed, and messing about with FI hybrids would be a nuisance. But in a year they would grow a lot. By the time they flowered next spring they would be quite sensational. She would show them at the Horticultural Hall. The pundits would give her hell for not keeping a proper record of what she had crossed with what, but they would be marvellous publicity for the new nursery.